Chasing the Tides

Bitsy Yates

World Castle Publishing, LLC
Pensacola, Florida
Copyright © 2025 Bitsy Yates
Hardback ISBN: 9798274955065
Paperback ISBN: 9798891264946
eBook ISBN: 9798891264953
First Edition World Castle Publishing, LLC, December 1, 2025
http://www.worldcastlepublishing.com

Cover: Cover Designs by Karen
Editor: Karen Fuller

Chapter 1

Newport, Rhode Island, Present Day: Charlotte

As Charlotte stepped off the airport bus, the sweet, salty air kissed her nose as if it had been there before. She repositioned the leather strap of her bag and walked forward while the soft waves of the harbor seemed to whisper her name.

"To your left is Bowen's Wharf, everything you need!" the driver exclaimed.

"*Everything* you need," Charlotte muttered to herself.

The rest of the passengers filed out, melting into the sea-soaked city that pulsed in time with the ocean, and the clang of buoys told her just how far she was from her hometown of Seattle. She noticed sailboats drifting lazily in the harbor, their hulls gently bumping against the dock.

She grazed her eyes over the bare landscape before stopping the first gentleman who walked as if he knew the land. "Sir, do you know where The Innlet is?"

"Yes ma'am, a few blocks up that street there." He pointed past grassy plots of boats covered in tarp. "Just keep walking until you stumble upon it. It should be on the right."

She hardly had time to thank him before he'd gone the other way, leaving her to be the only one to take the winding path up the hill. As excitement knotted in her belly, dread suddenly pulsed within her.

"Got it, thank you."

She trekked the hill as the buttery light of the rising sun slanted from cobblestone sidewalks, lighting them up like diamonds lived in their grains. Birds sang above her, drifting to and from trees hugging the road, the most magnificent green. Charlotte drew in a deep breath as her eyes slowly followed up to the top of Trinity Church. Newly blossomed flowers were waking from winter, and a cool, slight breeze brushed past her cheeks.

Newport had enchanted her ever since she was a child. Her grandparents used to live here before their deaths, just months apart. She could remember summers sailing with her grandfather or meeting the family downtown, eating all the seafood and oysters they could order. She hadn't been back since then, and when thinking of her next step, Rhode Island was the easy choice.

A few moments later, she came across a rustic building with the sign "The Innlet" adorning the front door. She swiftly walked inside, instantly greeted by a warm smile.

"Welcome!" the hostess pronounced, her fire engine red hair and eclectic jewelry made Charlotte smile.

"Hello, Charlotte Brooks," she lightly spoke, trying not to distract the woman in the corner reading.

"Yes, room 208. It has the loveliest view. If you find you need anything, please don't hesitate to let us know," she explained, sliding the room key across the desk.

"Thank you," Charlotte sweetly replied, grasping the key, turning towards the elevators.

She touched the key to the keypad and opened the heavy oak door. The quaint room was enveloped by a beautiful view of the harbor, sunshine streaming through the gauzy taupe curtains. Charlotte laid her bag on the edge of the bed, not taking her eyes off the view. She opened the sliding door onto her short patio, lifting her sunglasses to the top of her head. Her long skirt swayed with the breeze as her elbows found their home on the wooden ledge. At first glance, the spire of Trinity Church stole her eye. The birds chirping above her gave her a sense of serenity that she would never forget. After her tumultuous winter in the evergreen state, Charlotte desperately needed the calmness Newport already offered her. Nestled against the curve of the bay, the town felt like a secret tucked away from the rest of the world.

After a few moments of gratitude, Charlotte turned back inside. She opened her suitcase and organized her things in the small dresser below the television. When finished, she sat on her bed, thumbing through her social media.

He knew she was leaving, but he didn't know where. His Facebook and Instagram pages were quiet. She couldn't help but notice that he posted a picture from three months ago as if everything was fine.

Seeing his face put a sense of urgency inside Charlotte, and she ditched her flight clothes for cleaner attire, snatched her leather satchel, strapped on her shoes, and left the quiet room behind her to search for a job to officially tie her to this new life. She walked downstairs to the foyer of the hotel, noticing things she hadn't before. The exposed brick that had been a part of the original building in the 1800s warmed the room, the green plants added a pop of color, and the cozy leather lounge chairs seemed inviting. The latte machine brewed to life as its patrons made their first morning cup of hot coffee, its steam dancing above their mugs as they started their day. If there was a time to relax, it was now, especially after her long red-eye flight.

The street was quiet, and people moved slowly here. Charlotte could appreciate that. As she looked beyond the street, the ocean revealed itself, peeking from behind old homes and pink blossoming cherry trees. Charlotte was mindful of her feet, a slightly steep hill quickly moved her along.

Beautiful, she thought to herself as her tense shoulders softened.

As she crossed the street and returned to Bowen's Wharf, the shops and small restaurants bustled with life. A few patrons were window shopping and walking around, delighted by the sailboats docked at the pier. She came across a children's store, Finnegan's, a quaint little shop with small clothes and a nautical theme to appropriately match the sailboat town it was nestled in.

"Can I help you?" an older lady asked, as she folded a small blue and white onesie on the display case near the back of the store.

"Actually, yes," Charlotte started, "are you hiring? I just moved here and am looking for a job."

"We are always looking for someone ahead of the summer season. That seems to be our busiest. Let me get you an application and your phone number," she explained.

"I would very much appreciate that, thank you so much."

After a few minutes, she returned with an application, "My name is Debbie, if you need it, and I placed my phone number at the top here," she pointed out. "Just fill it out and bring it back."

"Will do," Charlotte grinned.

As she stepped back onto the small cobblestone side street, the sun warmed her nose. She couldn't remember the last time she had been this optimistic.

Coffee, she thought, *that's what I need.*

Charlotte continued to walk towards the water, a bookstore unfolding itself near the pier. The sign outside mentioned the latte of the day, a lavender vanilla iced coffee. Curiosity took over as she pushed the creaking door open, and the aroma of bitter coffee beans and fresh pastries filled the small room.

"Good morning," a cheery voice uttered, a frown curling into a smile.

"Morning," Charlotte said, noting the old books lining the walls.

"What can I get you?"

"Is that Lavender Vanilla iced coffee any good?" Charlotte asked.

"I think it's delicious," the barista beamed. "My little creation."

"I'll go with that then." She put down her card.

As she waited, Charlotte walked around, thumbing the dusty spines of the books illuminated by the sunlight streaming in from the large bay front window.

"Here you go!" the barista exclaimed, handing her the iced coffee. "Enjoy."

Charlotte carefully grabbed the iced drink and opened the straw that laid on top of it. After popping it into the top, she swished the ice around before taking a long sip.

Surprisingly good, she smiled.

The street outside was more crowded now. Charlotte sauntered towards the pier with her coffee in hand. She motioned the sunglasses over her eyes as the seagulls around her flew away, their wings fluttering. The blue cobalt skies matched the water, with little clouds in sight.

The perfect day to start fresh.

Seattle was so much busier. She thought she might miss the mountains and immense cedar trees, but this beautiful view and quaint town had quickly stolen her heart.

She took a deep breath, closed her eyes, and listened to the sounds around her. The low hum of rudders piddling through the harbor, the buoys bouncing between the foamy peaks of the small waves, and the horns of boats greeting those after a long night's work. It all seemed so simple, this life. Why had it seemed so complicated in the Pacific Northwest? She knew she had made the right decision by coming here, she felt it in her bones. Her marriage, which had ended, was so toxic to her life. She could see that now. At that moment, she felt she was free.

Away from the stress and away from *him*. Charlotte opened her eyes and took another long sip of her iced coffee.

Newport, she sighed, *show me how good it can be.*

Chapter 2

Newport, Rhode Island, Present Day: Charlotte

"When can you start?" Debbie asked, as soon as Charlotte handed her the application the next day.

"Is tomorrow too soon?" Charlotte asked.

"Perfect, see you at 8:00 am. There is no uniform, just dress in whatever you feel comfortable in."

"Sounds good, oh, and you can call me Charley," she explained. "Nobody has ever called me Charlotte."

"See you tomorrow then, Charley." With a sweet smile that made her feel like she was already home, Debbie swept behind the counter.

A tender optimism overwhelmed her. The pay wasn't much, but she had saved enough the past few years to get by for at least a year by herself. She knew this was just the beginning.

By mid-afternoon, Charlotte found herself exploring her new town a bit. She wanted to get to know her new home and become familiar with its obvious charm. Walking along Thames Street and peeking into stores, taking it all in. People were friendly here, and smiles were everywhere. As she left the storefronts, she wandered down streets aimlessly, passing the small signs on historic homes on Bellevue Avenue. Brightly colored pastel front doors, yellows, and reds livened the road. Fresh flowers in pots on people's porches, inviting hummingbirds and bees.

In her peripherals, she spotted an older lady having trouble walking up her front steps.

"I can help you," Charlotte offered, extending help.

"Oh, you don't have to," she chuckled, fumbling her keys in her shaking hands. The keys slipped through her grasp once, then after she picked them up, a second time. "Here, I can help with that." Charlotte gently picked them up and opened the front door.

"Thank you," she muttered, "I would have been here a few minutes. My carpal tunnel won't seem to go away." A heavy frown marred her forehead, and Charlotte quickly grazed her eyes over the woman's home to find something to make her smile.

Red tulips gathered in patches under the bay of her window, matching the crimson door. Charlotte gestured to it. "I love the color."

It worked. The woman brightened. "It's the original color. This home has been in my family for a century, and I want to preserve it." Now content, she lifted her weary gaze to Charlotte's and pushed the door open. "Would you like to come in? I am craving a cup of tea, if you're not busy."

"I would love that if I'm not imposing."

"Not at all, it's just me anyways," she said, "Susan, my name is Susan Mills, dear."

"Nice to meet you, I'm Charley," she extended her hand.

"That must be short for something," she winked, walking in the door and holding it open for her new guest.

"Charlotte Brooks, yes ma'am."

As they walked in, the old oak floors creaked with age, and Charlotte noticed the light and dark depressions and scratches that made it unique. The light gray walls accentuated the deep brown leather furniture, decorated with soft cashmere throw blankets and pillows.

"I just refinished the kitchen. Would you like to see it?" She motioned Charlotte to the left, just through the hearth of the small hallway.

Crisp white cabinets surrounded the upper walls, some with glass showing off Susan's blue and white Georgian plates. The island projected a pop of color, navy blue, which accentuated the speckled white marble countertops. A dream kitchen for any.

"It's beautiful here," Charlotte noticed out loud.

"The taxes aren't cheap," Susan snorted, placing her purse on the counter.

"You said you've been living here for how long?" Charlotte pried.

"Ever since I was a girl. I moved away but always found my way back home to Newport. When my parents passed, they left it to me. My husband died last year, so I've been tweaking things every so often with my grandson. It keeps me busy," Susan explained. "Where do you live?"

"I just arrived here yesterday, actually," Charlotte said, "I'm staying at a small hotel down the street."

"From where?"

"Seattle."

"How exciting." Susan's eyes widened. "You know, when I left here in my twenties, I had this hunger for travel. I didn't make it very far," she snickered, "but good for you for leaning into that. It takes a brave person to leave where life is comfortable."

"Not so sure about bravery, but I'm trying," Charlotte proceeded.

"May I ask what made you leave? My curiosity is getting the better of me," Susan urged, setting the teapot on the burner. Blue flames warming the bottom of the pot.

"I grew up there and am recently divorced," she shared.

"Sounds like this was a much-needed getaway," Susan said. "Do we want wine instead?" she winked.

"Probably," Charlotte laughed, "only if you're up for a long story."

"Honey, I'm always up for a story," she remarked, shutting off the burner.

Charlotte and Susan sat outside on her patio for three hours, swapping stories and sipping white wine, the teapot left cooling in the kitchen. The pink sunset filled the sky as they laughed and shared parts of their lives they didn't expect to share with a stranger. Their unexpected friendship sparked a light inside Charlotte that hadn't been bright in what seemed like a very long time. Susan was in her mid-seventies but still had lots of life left inside of her. Her eyes conveyed one filled with exciting moments and memories. She made Charlotte feel comfortable and important, something she didn't know she needed until it fell into her lap.

"So you start your new job tomorrow?" Susan asked, lifting her glass to her lips.

"Yes, 8:00 am, bright and early. I probably should

be going soon," Charlotte confessed. She could have stayed there all evening.

"Nonsense," Susan hushed. "What did you do for work in Seattle?"

"Public relations for a restaurant," she said. "It was a lot of fun, but kept me very busy. Wasn't exactly the job to have when starting a family," she divulged before stopping herself.

"Do you have any kids?" Susan inquired.

Charlotte paused, not sure how much she wanted to tell.

"No," she stated simply.

Susan's gaze flicked to her, then dropped. She'd told of her kids already, and if she hadn't noted Charlotte's silence then, her expression said that she noted it now. "It's getting late," Charlotte said, "I have an early morning."

"If you must," Susan sighed, embracing Charlotte in a warm hug. "I hope this town offers you the solace you need from whatever you run from."

Whatever you run from. Charlotte didn't mean to, but she dwelled on that line for far longer than she should have until her entire life in Seattle materialized before her eyes, until her head was spinning. She tried to shove it away as much as she could, but she knew she couldn't for long. She reminded herself this was her life and she was in control now, not *him*. As much as she wanted to, her past could not be erased. She could either choose to learn from it or let it paralyze her.

Charlotte shook her thoughts away as she let her new town comfort her. She opened her eyes to the few people walking back to their homes and heard soft laughter in the air. Gas lanterns lit up the cobblestone sidewalk, their flames dancing every which way. She had known nature to be beautiful, but the way she captured it now with a more optimistic perspective dazzled her. She had known the sun to bring light, but now noticed its beauty in more detail as it dipped beneath the horizon. Its golden haze stretched its arms in every direction, entangling the darkness and shadows with its charm, concealing its flaws. Who was she in the darkness, when all else had disappeared?

Charlotte waded through the waves in her mind and, with a sigh, navigated back to shore. She felt as if she had spent most of her life as a puppet, someone else always taking control of her strings. Charlotte realized now how deeply it had scolded her heart. Life did not have to be so linearly predictable, as she once believed. She did not have to follow the road that everyone else had been told to follow. Yet here, in the twilight of the evening, fireflies sprinkled dashes of joy into the darkness all around her. She decided to manifest their luminescence and light up the night, all on her own.

Once back at her hotel, she took a long, hot shower and cozied into a puffy bathrobe that was complimentary from the hotel. Her feet were warm, and so was her heart. Unexpectedly, she had made a new friend, and that had made all the difference.

Her hardened heart was starting to soften, but she knew it would take much longer than just making one friend. She wanted to keep the tough parts of her life in Seattle, not wanting it to bleed into her new life in the ocean state. She wanted to become a truer version of herself, one that was much different than her past. She vowed to learn from her mistakes and to try to break through the walls she had held up so high for so long in a marriage that had crushed her.

If she had never met *him,* life would have been so much different.

***

"Is someone sitting here?"

Charlotte looked up from her book to a tall, handsome man. She shifted in her seat and placed her book in her lap, gaining her composure.

"I don't think so," she replied, sitting straight up to look around at the empty seats around them.

Intrigued, she moved her bag to the other side of her seat, making room for him.

"Where are you headed?" he asked, smoothing down his button-down shirt as he got comfortable.

"Portland," she said, "and you?"

"Portland," he smiled.

The train signaled its departure and trudged forward. Charlotte noticed his pressed black sports coat and his colorful tie. He looked important, but also a little cocky.

"Is it really okay that I sit here? Or are you busy?" he said, glancing down at her book.

"As long as you're not a serial killer," she smirked.

"Not a serial killer," he assured her with a charming side smile, "is that what your book is about?"

"No," she giggled, curving her hair behind her ear.

"Henry James?" he looked at the cover, "never heard of him."

"He's underrated," Charlotte said, "one of my favorite authors, though. Are you a reader?"

"Sometimes," he confessed, "I haven't had the time recently."

"Life gets busy," she said, looking out the window.

"Asher," he said, extending his hand, "it's nice to meet you."

Charlotte glanced down at his hand, searching for a wedding band.

She didn't spot one.

"Charlotte," she said, their hands meeting, causing her cheeks to blush.

She noticed his firm yet gentle handshake.

"So, Portland," Asher said, "what brings you there?"

"Just visiting," she shared.

"Is your boyfriend meeting you there?"

"Not in the slightest," she said, rolling her eyes.

He nodded, appearing to consider her answer.

She didn't want to tell him she was going back to visit her mother. He was a stranger, she didn't feel the need to divulge those details of her life just yet.

"Would you like a drink?" he asked.

"Would love one," she nodded, nervously thumbing through the pages of her book that was still sitting on her lap.

Chapter 3

Newport, Rhode Island, Present Day: Charlotte

"Morning!" Debbie stated.

"Hello again," Charlotte remarked with a smile.

"Is that coffee from Mainsail?" she curiously asked.

"Yes!"

"Have you tried the Lavender Latte? Don't, it tastes like soap," Debbie smirked.

"I tried it the other day, it wasn't so bad," Charlotte answered truthfully.

"Okay, let's get started," Debbie announced.

After about an hour, Charlotte knew everything she needed to know about Finnegan's. Debbie was the proud owner and was very selective when hiring her staff. Only two other trusted employees worked there, after all, it was such a small shop. Debbie had moved to Newport from California a few years ago and decided she and her husband needed a change of scenery. She had three children, all grown and moved away, something she happily disclosed. She was a sweet woman and very confident about her business. She ran a tight ship. As long as you were on time and did your best, she was happy. Charlotte agreed to work four days a week, leaving her plenty of time to explore her new home and ultimately, herself.

Her shift ended a lot faster than she expected. She met and worked with another employee, Piper. Piper was younger than her but was helpful nonetheless.

"See you tomorrow," Piper said as she closed up the shop.

"Thank you for today, you made my first day go a lot smoother," Charlotte responded.

"No worries at all, I've been here a while, so it's second nature to me."

They parted ways, and Charlotte slowly made it back to her hotel. The evening was cool yet peaceful. Dogs were softly barking in the distance as cars rolled past her in the street. It wasn't until she reached her room that she opened her phone to see a missed call: *Asher.*

She decided after a shower and a glass of wine, she *might* be ready for that conversation. As she sat outside and enjoyed the sunset on her hotel balcony, Charlotte decided she didn't need to contact him right away. He had already taken so much from her that he didn't deserve much more. Her old self would have returned the call immediately, but she didn't have to give in like that anymore. She felt that maybe one day she would return his call, but tonight was not that night.

Instead, she looked online for a place to live. She knew she couldn't afford much, but an apartment or an extra room was exactly what she needed. She scrolled through the web and decided she would message a promising listing if she found one she liked. Someone nearby was renting their refinished basement, a one-bedroom, quaint little apartment with doors that led onto the street. It was only a moment from the Wharf, and you could not beat the price. After an hour, the lady who listed it sent her back a message asking to meet with her the next day. Charlotte agreed and decided to take a leap of faith. This place would be all her own, something nobody could take away. The excitement welled up inside of her, and a promise of another fulfilled day laid ahead of her.

She awoke the next morning to a knock at the door, subtle yet loud enough to wake her from her sleep. She jumped out of bed, pulled on her bathrobe, and quickly checked her hair.

A rat's nest.

Lovely.

She peeked through the door's peephole and pulled the handle open. A broad-shouldered man with a white doctor's coat and slacks was standing before her. He was holding a large coffee, a box of fresh croissants, and the biggest smile she'd ever seen.

"Hello?" Charlotte squeaked, her eyes had not had a chance to adjust to the morning light.

"You're not my fiancée," he said, looking her up and down with a quizzical look plastered on his face.

"That would be a no," she said.

She raked her tousled hair, instantly conscious of her haggard appearance.

"So sorry, um, I thought this was room 210," he fumbled, looking into her eyes a little longer than normal.

"208," Charlotte corrected him.

"Oh, I must have messed that up. So sorry to bother you," he said, turning to leave.

As he left, she poked her head out into the hallway, trailing him. He was very tall and attractive, she thought.

His dark hair accentuated his green eyes, his slender but tall physique lured her in, but something stopped her.

No, she remembered, *you are not ready for any of that.*

She turned, shutting the door behind her. She checked her phone.

7:15 am

It was her first day off, and she had a promising meeting about a new place to live. She decided it was a good time to shower and get ready for the day.

An hour later, she received a text from Susan.

Dinner tonight?

Charlotte had no other plans and responded that she wouldn't want to do anything else. It was true, she had such a fun time at their last meeting that it was no brainer. Plus, she figured she wasn't in a position to say no to a new friend.

She walked out onto the sidewalk and drew in a long breath. The air felt so pure and clean. It was an overcast day, but the sun was trying to sneak its way past the clouds. Birds soared above her, as a few people on bikes strode past. Their baskets were filled with fresh lilacs, a brilliant purple. Downhill, sailboats were slowly making their way into the harbor, their sails gently swaying in the morning wind. Her meeting was at 10:00, so she still had some time to herself. She figured she could grab a cup of coffee and a small bite to eat. She walked to Mainsail and ordered a small mocha latte and an oatmeal. It was delicious. She walked a bit towards the water, sat down on an open bench, and tapped on her iPhone screen that had been vibrating in her pocket: *Asher.*

"Yes?" she said, "You called yesterday."

"Well, hello to you, too," Asher blurted, clearly already

annoyed.

Charlotte instantly kicked herself for answering. Her old self was still making poor decisions inside of her.

"How's Rhode Island?" he asked.

"Beautiful, exactly what I—," she said as she stopped abruptly. She had not told him where she was headed. How did he know?

"I didn't think you would go," he confessed.

"Well, here I am," she insisted, "how can I help you?"

"Honestly, I was just calling to check up on you, to see how you were faring out there on the East Coast," he said.

"Really?" she asked, as her fingers pinched the bridge of her nose, her eyes shut.

"I mean, we may not be married anymore, but I still care about you."

"Sure," she exhaled.

"I can tell you're annoyed," he said, "just remember I'm only a phone call away if you need me."

"Got it," she said, tapping her screen, ending the call.

The audacity.

Was he charming? At times, yes. He knew when to turn it on and off, using his smile as a weapon. After five years, she decided she didn't want to battle life that way anymore. He charmed her at first, but after they got married, he let his true personality shine.

She pulled out a book from her leather satchel and opened it to the next chapter. The salty breeze brushed her hair in her face, and she gently curled her hair behind her ear. A big horn sounded directly in front of her, startling her. She had thought the boats before her were parked and unmanned.

Charlotte continued reading for a bit until she checked the small gold watch on her wrist. She stood up, pulling her light sweater down. She was only a few minutes away from the house. The breeze picked up as she rounded the corner to Thames Street. The road was busier than usual, probably the morning rush.

After a few minutes, she looked up as she came upon her destination, her possible new home. She walked up to the large wrap-around porch and marveled at the pale lavender door. Against the crisp white house, it looked marvelous. The homeowner had placed mauve and violet peonies close to the door, illuminating its beauty. Charlotte found the doorbell and gently pressed it. She slowly stepped back a bit, waiting for the door to open. When it did, a middle-aged woman answered the door with a smile.

"You must be Charlotte," she said. "Welcome!"

"Yes, hi, thank you for meeting with me. Your extra room looked too good to be true."

"Well, it's been refinished, but we never use it. We figured it was time to rent to someone. Let's go round back and I'll show it to you," she motioned, stepping out onto the porch and closing her front door.

"I love that color," Charlotte noted. "It's beautiful."

"Oh, thanks, the one that goes to the basement matches it. I'm Lydia, by the way," she said, offering her hand.

"Charley," she met her hand with hers.

"It's just this way," Lydia said, opening the small gate and leading Charlotte through the backyard.

As they turned, a lovely, matching purple door awaited them.

"Well, here it is," Lydia said, taking the key out of her pocket. She opened the door, and Charlotte marveled at the floors. They were refinished, and the scent of fresh paint filled the air.

"You can take a look around. Everything is new, the kitchenette isn't huge, but it has all your basics. There is one bathroom down that small hallway attached to the bedroom on your right," she explained.

Charlotte marveled at the fresh white walls and the natural light that radiated through the windows in the living room.

"It's lovely," Charlotte boasted.

"We just ask no painting, but you can hang up and decorate as you wish," Lydia said.

"How much are you asking for rent again?" Charlotte inquired.

"$2,000 a month," Lydia offered, "I know one other person was looking at it yesterday, so all I ask is that if you want it, you pay your first month's rent up front. We do have a short rental agreement we would like you to sign, but that's it. Rent is due on the first of every month."

Charlotte took a quick peek into each room, then reappeared. "I'll think it over and get back to you."

She stood there for a moment, frozen, eyes wide in disbelief. A warm flush crept slowly up her neck and onto her cheeks. She had saved up a good amount of money before leaving Seattle, but if she paid that rent every month, she wouldn't be here long.

"We'll be in touch soon," Lydia said, handing her the paperwork and leading Charlotte outside.

"Thank you," Charlotte said with a tight smile.

She glanced down at the paperwork before tossing it away in a nearby trash can. She sighed and decided to find solace with the ocean, after all, she was close to the Cliff Walk. After a few moments of wandering toward the main road, strolling past red tulips, she began to see green signs pointing her in the ocean's direction. Several blocks later, she heard the rumbling of waves crashing against the rocky shore. The breeze picked up as she crossed her arms in an attempt to warm herself. As she looked up, the ocean view stole her attention as she stepped forward. The sun cast a beautiful golden hue atop the waves, explicating its beauty. She turned her attention to the runners on the slim pathway, as if they were gliding above the cliffs. Charlotte walked over to the railing, her face cradled in her hands. She stared out onto the bluffs as if at any moment, the sky would overtake her.

She felt a sudden wave of happiness amongst the unknown. A new place to live and a non-stressful job were exactly what she yearned for. She willed herself to be proud of venturing outside her comfort zone.

***

Charlotte savored her generous glass of white wine as Asher sipped his crisp, cold beer. Their conversation over the past three hours had been effortless, just as their train had glided upon its tracks. Their obvious chemistry simmered as they laughed and talked. Charlotte enjoyed his quick wit while he was enamored with her soft smile.

"How long are you in Portland for?" Asher asked.

"Just a few days," she said.

"Would you be free for dinner tomorrow by chance?" he

asked.

"I think I could get away," she smiled.

"I'm here for business, but have nothing planned for tomorrow night. I know a place you might like," he said, noticing their entrance into the Portland station. "Can I have your number?"

"Sure," she said, putting her contact information in his iPhone. "There you go."

"I'll see you tomorrow, Charley," he grinned.

"See you," she said, sliding the book she barely opened back into her bag.

He winked at her as he stood up to grab his belongings, which weren't much. A briefcase and a duffel bag were all he had with him. A simple man, she had thought.

Charlotte was optimistic, but not naive. She was hopelessly romantic to her core, but felt she was very aware of her emotions at this point in her life. She did not want to think much about it, knowing this could end up just being another failed date. However, a small part of her mind had hope. Hope that this person who unexpectedly dropped into her life might be able to change it. He could be the man she had been waiting for, the man she would live the rest of her life with. The possibility of that excited her, and she decided she would keep an open mind.

Chapter 4

Seattle, Washington, One Year Prior

Charlotte placed her large mug of coffee on her kitchen island as she took a seat on the wooden barstool hiding underneath the counter. Her coffee was heavily creamed with a splash of cubed sugar, her favorite. She needed something to brighten her day after her morning meeting with her lawyer. The divorce was messy, not that she had anticipated anything different. Asher didn't seem to want to let go of certain things. For example, he wanted their large oak kitchen table and all of its chairs, both of their cars, their wedding photo album, and other minuscule things. She couldn't understand why he wanted their wedding photo album, but she was able to let that go. She didn't, after all, want those memories to stain her independent life. His arrogant and forceful personality clashed with Charlotte's lawyer, and Charlotte didn't want to prolong the divorce any further. She planned to move across the country anyway, so it didn't hurt her to part with any of those materialistic items.

She stared outside her large kitchen window while her computer fired up. The rain was steady, and a soft mist hovered over the thick branches of the cedar trees across the bay. The morning was heavy with a thick blanket of opaque clouds that seemed to press down on the small town of Bainbridge

Island. A ferry ride away from the city, it was nestled on its island, away from the chaos. On a good day, you could make out the famous needle from her family room window. Asher was hesitant about living there because it would make his commute longer, but they both couldn't resist their small but quaint log cabin. It had views of both the bay and the ocean, depending on which window you looked out, making the morning and evening sky its own entertainment.

She drew in a hesitant breath as she opened an email from her lawyer.

She read the subject line, and a smile quickly formed on her face. Asher had finally signed the papers that morning at his lawyer's office. After moving out to an apartment in the city a year ago, she didn't know why he was dragging his feet after he expressed so much disdain for her and their marriage at their last meeting. She had initiated the divorce and was ready to move on, but he still seemed tied to it. It was his need to control her narrative that he craved; this divorce highlighted that. They agreed that he would get the house and the specific items he wanted inside of it, and she would get what was left of their shared trust fund. It wasn't much, maybe that was why he had agreed.

She had been set free.

"Where to next?" her lawyer texted her moments later.

"Rhode Island," Charlotte confidently replied.

***

Newport, Rhode Island, Present Day: Charlotte

Charlotte wore the dress that her husband never liked, along with the tan heels that made her feel invincible.

She regretted the shoes as she made the steep walk to the bookstore, holding her iced coffee, but her reflection in the windows, as she passed shops, told her the pain was worth it. It was almost like looking into the past. The girl she saw there was confident, prepared, and not at all heartbroken. If she stared long enough, she almost believed her heartbreak to be gone.

As she watched, a familiar face appeared behind her. Charlotte swiftly turned around to see the man from that morning, in jogging shorts and sneakers. He wore a navy blue windbreaker to cut the breeze while he ran. He spotted her and paused.

"Hi?" she said, confused.

"Are you following me?" he laughed, his green eyes twinkling as the sun started to shine behind him.

"Umm, no," she babbled, not sure what to say.

"I'm just kidding, it's a small town," he grinned. "Wes," introducing himself.

"Charlotte, well, Charley," she mumbled.

"Which is it?"

"Charley, sorry, nobody calls me Charlotte," she said, shaking his hand. She winced as their fingers touched, highly aware that she'd just offered the cold hand that held her drink, but his crooked smile said that he took no note of it. His touch lingered.

"Are you from here? I figured not since you're at a hotel."

Had he been thinking of me? Charlotte took her hand back to hold her drink. "Just moved here from Seattle," she said with more confidence.

"Welcome to Newport. It's a little different here on the East Coast, huh?"

"Yes, but it's beautiful," she said, looking out onto the water.

"Can't deny that," Wes said, their eyes lingering a moment before the other spoke.

"Well, you get going on your run," she said. "It was nice to meet you…again."

"Agreed," Wes said. "Have a great day."

Charlotte turned back to walk up the path to the main road and checked her watch. Maybe she could surprise Susan a little earlier.

She turned the corner to her street and noticed the mailman slipping mail into Susan's mailbox beside her door. Once on the steps, Charlotte grabbed it for her and lightly knocked. The woman opened it with a warm smile.

"I was hoping it was you." Susan welcomed her in as she pulled the apron from around her neck, folding it into a neat pile that she laid the mail upon. Flour dusted the shoulders of her floral blouse, and sugar was sprinkled over her thin slippers.

"I know I'm early." Charlotte closed the door behind her and slipped off her heels.

"What's an old lady like me got to do anyway?" She gestured her further into the home, where the scent of pumpkin pie greeted them. She raised a brow. "Pumpkin pie at this time of the year?"

Susan chuckled. "It's always a good time for pumpkin pie."

Charlotte pulled out a chair in the dining room,

glancing at the oven. "Can't argue with that. It certainly fills the home with a wonderful smell."

"Speaking of homes," Susan said as she eased into a chair beside Charlotte. "Find a place to live?"

"Kind of, but I'm not sure I can swing it," Charlotte said. "It's a small place just around the corner, but she's asking $2,000 a month."

"Nonsense," Susan said. "Why don't you save your money and live here with me? I have plenty of open rooms upstairs."

"Oh, I wouldn't want to…" Charlotte started.

"Bother me?" Susan guessed. "Never, I would love the company anyway. You are freshly divorced, save your money!"

Charlotte paused, contemplating her request.

"Oh, come on, it would be fun," she winked. "It's really quiet around here, and I won't bother you. My grandson comes over from time to time to help me around the house, but other than that, it's just me…and my book club night with my girlfriends."

"Okay," Charlotte said. "As long as I'm not imposing."

"I'm excited!" Susan beamed. "Gather your things at the hotel tonight and come over in the morning. I'll get you settled before work."

"Okay," Charlotte said.

"How's work anyway? Meet anyone new?" Susan questioned. A devilish gleam sparked in her eyes.

Charlotte paused for a moment, taking a sip of tea. She could feel the cold river make its way down to her empty stomach.

"Actually, yes," Charlotte said, keeping her tone flat. "I keep bumping into someone. He mistakenly showed up at my door the other morning, thinking it was his fiancée's room, and then again on a run."

Susan's eyes widened.

"He was wearing a white coat this morning, but then I saw him on a run."

"Oh, a doctor? My grandson's a doctor, too. He sometimes works night shifts at the hospital. He adores the children," she continued, looking off into the distance. "I hate his fiancée, though. He could have done so much better if you ask me," she said begrudgingly. "There are no pictures of that woman in my house." Her tone turned stiff.

"What's her name?" Charlotte asked.

"Her name is Emily," Susan explained. "They were childhood friends, met in diapers pretty much. Her family has a lot of money, Dad's the Governor of Rhode Island, and her mom grew up with my daughter."

"I see," Charlotte said. "When is their wedding?"

"Near Christmas," Susan remembered, her eyes looking up to the ceiling as she thought. "Quite a few months away."

Charlotte smiled, taking another long sip of her tea, "What about you?" she asked. "Have anything...or anyone... going on?"

"Just went on a date last night," she mocked.

"Really?" Charlotte said, surprised.

"Absolutely not," Susan laughed. "You'll catch on to my sarcasm sooner or later."

The two laughed all afternoon until it was time for

Charlotte to leave. Instead of walking back to the hotel, she decided to take a detour, walking a little farther down different windy roads she hadn't yet been to. The silence was eerie yet optimistic. She felt alone but not scared; she was beginning to be able to spend time with herself. It had been a long time since she had been able to enjoy the silence. Her thoughts seemed to shift like the slow-moving tide–first, the corners of her mouth twitched upward, as if she could taste the happier days. But then, her smile faded, her brows furrowed slightly as the darker memories came into focus. She thought back to pain, loss, and the times she stumbled and fell. The path that she thought was clear had turned uncertain and jagged.

The past had such a hold on me, she sighed. *It's exhausting.*

Charlotte's jaw tightened, and a subtle tension emerged in her shoulders as if she were being pulled by an invisible force. There was a hesitation in her movements, like she was caught between two worlds, unsure whether to move forward or to turn back.

I have to let certain people go, she thought.

***

Newport, Rhode Island, Present Day: Wes

"Well, you're all sweaty," Emily mocked, resting her arms on Wes's shoulders.

"Yeah, went on a great run though," he admired.

"Wasn't it chilly?" she asked, her mouth scrunching up to her nose.

"Not when you're running," he smirked.

"Well, shower and get ready, we'll be late to brunch with my parents," Emily insisted.

"I may skip out on that; my shift last night was long, and I had to perform extensive surgery. Do you think they would mind if I didn't make it this time?" Wes asked, hoping for the best.

"You're not coming with me? Please…I was counting on you," she whined.

"I want to go, but I'm exhausted, plus I have to go back in tonight," he explained.

"You weren't too exhausted for a long run."

He frowned as he shucked off his jacket. "That relaxes me." *Your parents do not.*

"Just drink some coffee, you'll be fine."

Wes shrugged and walked up the steps to his room, where his steaming shower awaited him. Frustration curled in his chest. He was drained, mentally and physically, from the surgery from yesterday, and his thoughts still lingered on the young boy who'd barely survived it, much less recovered. Wes made a mental note to check in on him once his shift started that night. The young boy deserved that.

His mind wandered as the scorching water hit his skin. Wes stood there a moment, his hands against the shower wall, his head resting on his shoulders.

Charley. What an interesting name, he thought.

***

"You look beautiful," Asher said, holding the door to the restaurant open for her.

"Thank you," Charlotte beamed.

"Good evening, Mr. Bradford," the hostess smiled, "right this way."

"They know you here," Charlotte commented.

Asher laughed to himself, "I come here a lot for business."

"I see," Charlotte said.

The waitress walked them to their table in the back corner of the spacious dining room.

"Will this suit you?" the hostess asked.

"Yes, thank you," Asher nodded.

They both took their seats, both nervously glancing at one another and the menu.

"What do you recommend?" Charlotte asked.

"Anything, honestly," he said.

As Charlotte looked at the menu and then back at Asher, she noticed his attention was elsewhere. He was staring. Staring so intently at something or someone behind her. Her nerves grew, but she didn't want to show it.

"Everything okay?" Charlotte whispered.

He didn't answer at first; his concentration had been stolen.

"Yes," he muttered, closing the menu and placing it on the edge of the table. "You know, this place is kind of stuffy for a first date, don't you think?" he asked.

"Umm," Charlotte murmured.

"Let's go somewhere else, you want to?"

Asher started to stand as Charlotte looked around her. The other patrons, thankfully, paid no mind to them. Yet, Charlotte felt a wave of anxiousness.

"Okay," she said, standing up and grabbing her clutch.

As she followed Asher back to the front of the restaurant, she quickly glanced over her shoulder to see what he had been so transfixed with. She knew immediately. A beautiful woman who had been sitting behind her was staring back at her, a glass of red wine placed up to her burgundy lips. Her light brown hair cascaded *down her shoulders, a small smirk on her face.*

Charlotte quickly turned back, following him out to the busy Portland street.

"Asher?" she asked. "What is this about?"

"Nothing," he said, continuing to walk forward.

"I don't play games, and I don't get involved in complicated situations. Is there someone I need to know about?" she said, stopping in the middle of the busy sidewalk.

Asher turned around, a look of pain on his tense face, reluctant to tell her.

"I saw her," Charlotte said. "Who was she?"

Wes looked away, avoiding the question.

"Fine," Charlotte said, turning to walk away.

"Someone from my past," he said. "I think she was there to ruin this, our date," he said, ashamed.

Charlotte stole a look behind her. She couldn't see her now, but from the confident draw of her shoulders as the two left, she'd accomplished exactly what she'd come for. And from the sloped draw of Asher's eye, it gutted him to see her. Something within her drew her to his side, where she stroked a hand up his arm. Encouraged by the touch, he brightened. "Why was that so hard to tell me?" she asked.

"I don't care to talk about things in my past," he said. "Is there any way to salvage this date?"

Charlotte paused, looking at him straight in the eyes, a small smile curling the corners of her lips. The woman in the restaurant would not win. Charlotte would turn this date around and make it the best one there was.

"Ice cream," she grinned.

Chapter 5

Seattle, Washington, Two Years Prior

"I just want to pop in," Charlotte pleaded. "They are having their annual sale, it won't take long."

"Fine," Asher huffed, turning down a busy street. "Jump out, I'll find a parking spot and find you in there."

"Thank you!" Charlotte smiled.

As she walked into her favorite clothing boutique, its bright lights and trendy soft music lured her in. Charlotte browsed through a rack of dresses, holding up a few to herself as she examined the fit. Asher appeared a few moments later, his hands stuffed into his pockets.

"What do you think about this one?" she asked, holding up the dress next to her silhouette.

Asher thumbed through the other dresses hanging on the rack and plucked a different one, handing it to her. His eyes widened.

"This one's perfect for you, you could definitely pull it off."

Charlotte laughed, a little flattered, but also hesitant. Its plunging neckline and bright red color intimidated her, far more daring than her usual taste.

"I don't know, I was thinking of something simpler."

Charlotte glanced at the dress again, biting her lip.

"I really think you would look amazing in this," he said.

She folded it over her arm as she walked about, her eyes still uncertain. They walked around the store together, and as they passed a pair of shoes Charlotte had been eyeing, Asher quickly picked them up and handed them to her.

"These are wonderful, you should get these too," his voice smooth and convincing, almost too easy.

Charlotte hesitated but took them anyway, knowing they were way out of her price range.

"Maybe this is all too much," Charlotte said, thumbing the price tag on the red dress.

"You never splurge on yourself, babe, don't sell yourself short. Someone as incredible as you deserves to treat themselves."

A small wave of discomfort washed over her as her smile flickered out. Asher's words were persuasive, tugging at her emotions. She slowly nodded, walking up to the counter.

"Oh, these earrings are beautiful, get these too," he said, placing them next to the dress and shoes.

"Will that be all?" the clerk asked.

"Yes," Charlotte said.

Asher's arm securely rested on her waist as she watched the clerk ring up her items. She couldn't help but notice how easily he had steered her towards items she hadn't planned on buying. The dress, shoes, and earrings seemed to be his idea more than hers.

Charlotte's hand hovered over her wallet as she waited for the total.

"You sure this isn't too much?" she whispered to

Asher.

"No, use my card," he said. "I wouldn't want you to max yours out."

She hesitated for a long moment, a strange feeling prickling her skin. She swiped *his* card, and as the purchases went through, the transaction felt hollow.

It's like she had been swept along a current, without even realizing it.

***

Newport, Rhode Island, Present Day: Charlotte

Charlotte awoke the next morning, feeling refreshed and ready for the day. She got dressed, pulled her hair into a bun atop her head, and grabbed the last of her belongings.

"Morning!" the front desk clerk exclaimed as Charlotte drifted down the stairs.

"Good morning," she grinned.

"Leaving us?" the front desk clerk asked.

"Yes, but not going far," Charlotte said. "Just down the road."

"Well, if you don't need anything else, we will charge the card on file for you."

"Thank you," Charlotte replied.

It was a little brisk outside, but her cardigan gave her upper body some warmth. As she walked down the street, a few fallen white petals rushed into the air with the wind as joggers quickly ran through them. The harbor peeked behind the trees and houses as she made her way to her new, temporary home.

As she approached the door and raised her hand to

knock, it swung open, revealing Susan, her lips curled into a smile.

"Welcome home," she said.

"Good morning," Charlotte smiled.

"Follow me, honey, I'll show you to your room." Susan turned, shutting the door behind them.

"Thank you," Charlotte said as they both climbed the stairs.

"Here is where you can stay," Susan paused, opening the door to the first room on the right. "There are always fresh linens in the hall closet if you need them."

So much natural light streamed in through the French doors on the opposite side of the room. Beyond it, a little patio overlooked the harbor with a perfect view. She could already see herself having coffee outside every morning, journaling and gazing at the morning sun, and hearing the boats honking coming back into the harbor from off into the distance.

"Thank you," Charlotte said, placing a few things on the bed.

"Well, you get settled and I'll be downstairs," Susan said, placing a kind hand on Charlotte's shoulder before leaving. "When is work?"

"An hour," Charlotte said, glancing down at her watch.

"I made lunch if you want a bite before leaving," she offered.

"I will, thank you, really, you are far too kind. Especially to a complete stranger."

"You're not a stranger any longer, my dear," Susan said, closing the door.

An hour later, with a fuller belly and brighter heart,

Charlotte made her way to work. The harbor slowly came into view as she walked down the hill, the sailboats and fishermen coming in and out of the harbor. Seagulls and Osprey were flying around Bowen's Wharf, as if on their way to work too. It was unfolding into such a beautiful scene. Moments later, Charlotte climbed the brick steps to the shop's entrance.

"Good news?" Debbie asked from behind the counter.

"I'm not homeless!" Charlotte announced.

"Well, that's good," she laughed. "Now, a new shipment came in last night. Can you unbox, tag, and organize them on the floor?" she asked, getting straight to business.

"Sure thing," she said, placing her things behind the counter and swiftly making her way to the back of the store.

Today could not get any better.

***

Newport, Rhode Island, Present Day: Wes

"Dr. Novell, you have a patient in room one."

"Thanks, Tiffany," he said, returning to his office.

Wes placed his things on the wall hanger and powered up his laptop, quickly shuffling out the door to see his first patient of the day.

"Dr Novell?" A small face smiled, her eager parents beaming beside her.

"Angie!" Wes smiled, closing the door behind him, "My unofficial favorite patient."

A bright, cheery-eyed little girl smiled on the patient table, extending her arms to Wes. He quickly put his things down and gathered her in for a hug. Angie Stillman and her parents were easily the nicest people in the world. They were always respectful and patient, even with Angie's aggressive Leukemia diagnosis. They have always tried to be strong for Angie, yet very protective of their little girl. Wes felt a deep connection to Angie. Her willingness to advocate for herself and ask questions about her treatment always stunned him.

"She's been doing a little bit better since her last chemo treatment," Angie's mother smiled. "Without you, we wouldn't be here today."

"Oh, you don't have to say all of that," Wes charmed, patting Angie lightly on her head, "how are you feeling?"

"A little better," the six-year-old said, "sometimes my stomach hurts."

"We had her latest chemo treatment about one week ago," her father added, "sometimes nausea hits out of nowhere."

"Unfortunately, that's normal, but if you take those nausea meds, it'll help a bit," Wes explained, "let me check some things out and go over your last scan with you."

Angie nervously fidgeted on the patient's table, the sanitary paper crinkling underneath her, as they anxiously awaited the results.

"Okay," Wes sighed, "the cancer hasn't spread anywhere, that's the good news. Remember, there is no timeline, as cancer can be unpredictable, but I'm hopeful."

"Hopeful?" Angie's mother repeated, asking for reassurance.

"Right now, we are in good shape. You still have a few more chemo treatments scheduled until your next scan, so let's just continue to monitor and treat symptoms as they come," he said, noticing Angie's mood declining.

"Hey," he said, lifting Angie's chin upward, "you are one of the strongest little girls I know. You got this."

"Thanks," she sighed, hugging her teddy bear against her chest.

"Mom, Dad, you know where to find me," he said, extending a handshake to Angie's parents.

As they hugged and left the room, Wes sighed and turned to his laptop. He knew his job was difficult, but sometimes he wished his heart wasn't as big as it was.

Chapter 6

Newport, Rhode Island, Present Day: Charlotte

As Charlotte unloaded the dishwasher in Susan's kitchen, her cell phone dinged, signaling a text message's arrival.

If you're up for it, a few of us from the store are meeting up for live music down at the Wharf. We would love for you to join us! – Debbie

Charlotte's eyes darted to the clock hanging in her kitchen.

Be there in 20 minutes – Charlotte

There was nothing like live music and a few cocktails to welcome the summer season. It was getting closer, and everyone around town noticed it. More outdoor events were popping up, and people who fled Newport in the cooler months were beginning to arrive once again, ready for long days by the ocean with family and friends. She would be a part of that culture now, and a large smile drew across her face.

She kept her jeans on but threw on a light olive jacket over her shoulders to keep her warm by the harbor. She slid into her cognac leather mules, gathered her purse, and locked the charming crimson door behind her. As she strolled down the road, she could already hear the sounds of live music in the distance. The tangerine sun was slowly setting, turning the clouds a beautiful amber. Birds sputtered around the sky, finding their resting place for the night. As she turned the corner, Bowen's Wharf was bustling with life. The cobblestoned Thames Street embraced her as if to greet her arrival. Soft white twinkle lights adorned the shops and restaurants, and tables outside were filled with people talking and laughing. She stopped to take it all in; it was absolutely beautiful. The harbor was behind it all, its dark water a mirror to all the lights.

"Charley!" She heard, looking off to the side. She spotted Debbie and Piper waving to her, another person she hadn't recognized sitting beside Piper, smiling.

"Hey guys," Charlotte laughed, getting a quick hug from Debbie and Piper.

"Seth!" the younger man smiled, offering his hand.

"Charley," she laughed. "Nice to meet you."

"You haven't worked with Seth yet; he works off hours for us and covers if we need him to," Debbie explained.

"Want a drink?" Piper asked, lifting her empty glass.

"What are you having? It looks delicious," Charlotte nodded.

"Spicy margarita, I highly recommend it," Piper beamed.

"Yes, please!"

Piper got up and headed for Diego's, a Mexican restaurant next to their table. Its open bar faced them, with easy access to its patrons.

"They *are* good," Debbie insisted.

Charlotte scanned the large patio, where all types of people gathered around large and small black iron tables.

Many were laughing, drinking, and swapping stories of their week. It was cheerful and delightful. In Seattle, the streets were filled with people walking fast, faces tucked into phones, and mouths permanently turned down. It would be a struggle to find a scene like this there. Here, friendliness was the heartbeat of the town.

As if he read her thoughts, Seth said, "I heard you just moved from Seattle." He took a sip of his drink.

"I did, a long journey for sure," Charlotte sweetly smiled, adjusting her jacket.

"Here you go," Piper nudged, placing a spicy margarita in front of her, a jalapeno slice floating atop the ice.

"You didn't have to do that," Charlotte reminded her.

"Oh, stop, consider it your welcoming present."

Charlotte took a long sip, its sweet and spicy flavors bursting on her tongue. "You are onto something with these," she grinned, taking another long sip.

"Told you," Piper smirked, lifting her glass to cheers Charlotte.

"So who's playing tonight?" she asked, looking around.

"Wes Novell, he's a local but does live shows from time to time," Debbie resolved.

"Wait. Wes? As in the doctor?" Charlotte asked, dumbfounded.

"Yeah, he's getting married to this pill of a girl," Piper snickered, "I went to school with them growing up, he's a really good singer."

Charlotte scanned the crowd for Susan. She knew she had plans with one of her friends, but was hoping to see her here. She wasn't expecting this to be a town event, but by the way people were streaming in, it seemed like the beginning of many nights under the Wharf lights.

A few moments later, Wes took the small stage with two other gentlemen. He sat on the stool that was situated in front of the mic and looked so calm and comfortable. He positioned his guitar and looked out into the crowd with a big smile on his face.

"Hey guys," he said, lightly strumming his guitar. "Tonight I figured I'd play some of my favorites, but I am open to any suggestions. Just enjoy and relax."

As he started playing, his voice softly followed, slightly startling Charlotte. The tenderness in his voice brought chills up her spine.

He could sing, she thought.

Charlotte looked at Piper.

"Right?" Piper grinned as if she could read her mind.

The audience quieted as they listened, Wes' music filled the Wharf like the tide saturating the sandy beach. Everyone was enjoying themselves, and so was Charlotte. She couldn't imagine where she would be right now if she weren't in Rhode Island. Its people and lifestyle seemed to suit her.

"Did you get all moved into your new place?" Debbie asked.

"Getting there, it's just so nice to have a warm home again," Charlotte confessed.

The crowd started to mingle, people's voices rising just a tad, but still soft enough to hear Wes.

"Funny to see you here," a familiar voice inquired, tapping Charlotte's shoulder.

"Hey, Susan!" Charlotte glimmered, offering a hug.

"Enjoying the entertainment?" Susan winked.

"Better than I thought," Charlotte divulged. "Guys, this is my friend, Susan."

"Oh, hello!" They all said delightfully.

"Hi, everyone," Susan said, a huge smile on her face.

"Care to join us?" Debbie asked.

"Oh, thank you, but my gaggle of friends is waiting for me over there," she pointed. "Enjoy, it was nice to meet you guys," she smiled, lightly pinching Charlotte's shoulder, in a playful way, "I'll see you later, dear."

Charlotte turned her chair so she could get a better look at Wes. The night was clear, the stars slowly appearing from behind the few lingering clouds in the sky. His khaki shorts and light blue button-down made his blue eyes pop, his brown leather boat shoes tapping as he played. She hadn't noticed it before, but the dark lines of a tattoo dipped below his forearms. Her eyes followed them as he gently strummed his guitar. The black ink etched onto his skin weaved together what she assumed to be his life's memories and stories. She made out the shaded tentacles of an octopus, assuming it continued up to cover the rest of his arm. Only half of it was visible, the start of a story she wanted to know more about. Charlotte couldn't help but notice how attractive he really was. Yes, he could sing, but it was the way he strummed his guitar so delicately that drew her in.

"Ready for work tomorrow?" Debbie interrupted.

"You work with me tomorrow," Piper smiled."Bright and early."

Charlotte's phone lit up.

Asher

"Who's Asher?" Piper prodded.

"That's a long story," Charlotte muttered.

***

"I want you to know," Asher explained. "I saw this night going much different."

"You don't have to explain," she said, licking her ice cream cone as they walked.

"Well, still, I feel bad," he said,

"No need to," she said. "I'm fully aware people have their pasts."

"What about you? Any crazy ex-boyfriends?" he asked.

"Not worthy enough to mention," she said, biting down on her cone.

They chatted as they walked. Charlotte tied the waist of her jacket towards her chest, the coldness of the ice cream lowering her temperature. The night was beautiful, and the stars were clear.

"Look at that," Asher said, walking towards the Willamette River.

The water glistened under the bustle of downtown Portland. The golden city lights glimmer on top of the water as if to shine a light, signifying its beauty. Asher stopped at the railing, in amazement at its beauty.

"I can't decide if I like it here or Seattle more," he said.

Charlotte looked at him intently. She saw the emotion in his eyes, the gentleness of his demeanor. He seemed so kind, yet almost too good to be true. His cell phone suddenly rang, and a pang in Charlotte's heart emerged.

Was it her? She thought that mystery woman in the restaurant.

"Yes, I'll be right there," he said into the phone.

"Everything okay?" she asked, resting her arms on the railing.

"I have to run back to the office; something needs my immediate attention."

"Oh, okay," Charlotte said, trying to mask her sadness at their abrupt separation.

"I will text you, though. When do you go back to Seattle?" he asked.

"Tomorrow afternoon," she said. *"Quick trip."*

"Okay," he said. *"I'll be sure to speak with you soon, I promise."*

He placed a light kiss upon her cheek before turning to leave.

Charlotte paused and looked out at the river once again. She could hear the soft ripples of waves as the water trailed along. She would be lying if she didn't feel upset that their date had been cut short, but there was nothing she could do. She realized that he was a hard worker, but it made her weary. He was so quick to leave her, all alone in the heart of the city late at night. She allowed herself to look into her future for a moment. Would his job commitments be more important than her? She knew he was important to his business, but would he be able to draw a line between his personal and professional life? She didn't want to fall in love with someone so quickly, only to be chosen second.

Was he capable of juggling both?

****

Seattle, Washington, Two Years Prior

Charlotte and Asher were enjoying their lattes at their local coffee shop, one that was quaint and cozy. She had been struggling with a decision for weeks, taking the promotion her restaurant manager offered her, or moving on and doing something else. She peered at him over her laptop, her nose twitching with anxiousness. He knew of the promotion, but wasn't aware of how much it affected her. She had been asking her family and friends, but everyone had their own opinion, making it harder for her to decide. He was reading an article in the newspaper when he crinkled its center, noticing her stare.

"Yes?" he asked.

"I still don't know what to do," she said.

"Believe it or not, but I've been thinking a lot about your situation," he said.

"You have?"

"Yes. I think you should stay and take the promotion. You have marketed and made that place millions of dollars; it's time to reap the rewards."

He made sense, but there was a pang of regret that started to blossom in her chest.

"But haven't you wondered what it would be like if we moved somewhere else? Started a new adventure?"

Asher set his newspaper down on the table, his eyes on his wife. He leaned in slightly, his tone lowering to something more intimate.

"Start over?" he said.

"Yeah, wouldn't it be exciting? We've lived here a while, and I just feel it in my bones that we need a change," she explained.

"We?" he asked.

Charlotte fidgeted with her cup, unsure how to voice her concerns.

"Yes. It's no mystery that things between us have been different."

"I'm sorry, is this when you ask for couples counseling?" he asked sarcastically.

"What? No, I just—" she started to say, but couldn't finish the sentence.

"Charlotte, come on, everyone feels the pressure of what others expect of them. That is no reason to run from it."

"I've been feeling this for a while," she said. "I just haven't been able to bring it up to you."

"Let's think logically for a second," he said, immediately dismissing her feelings as quickly as she said them. "Think about how much you'll regret it if you don't take this opportunity? I mean, the compensation package alone went up significantly. You are finally going to be paid what you deserve. If we leave now, you may never find that again," he explained.

There was something in his words, something she had heard before—just a little differently–whispering into her own mind.

"But that's it," she said. "What if better is out there?"

"Don't think like that. You've been killing it here, don't lose it all now."

Charlotte took a deep breath, her heart racing. His words were so full of confidence and so convincing. She'd been wavering between the two choices for weeks, so taking the promotion would easily put it all to rest. But now, sitting here with Asher, it almost felt like the right decision was the one she'd been avoiding, the one where she takes the leap. The fear she felt lingered in the air between them, but the rush of possibility overshadowed Asher's continued reasons to stay.

"Don't waste any more time," he said. "You know what to do."

Chapter 7

Newport, Rhode Island, Present Day: Charlotte

Charlotte groggily awoke, her cheeks clenched, noticing her dry mouth. She reached for her phone; she had only 25 minutes until she had to be at work. With a groan, Charlotte rolled over and kicked the blankets off her, extending a leg to the cold hardwood floor. She slowly made her way to her shower, with no intention of blow-drying her hair. The warm water tingled her skin, and she could feel herself coming back to life.

As she dressed herself, she could hear the bluebirds in their nest just outside her window. A few chirps interrupted her thoughts from last night. A memory flashed before her eyes, Wes smiling at *her* as she turned to leave last night, her own laughter lingering in the space between them.

What happened? She thought. She remembered Piper saying they were working together, maybe she would be able to fill Charlotte in.

She slipped on her black leggings, her blue and white striped button-down, and white sneakers. She pulled her wet hair back into a low bun and clasped it with a large claw clip, grabbed her phone and leather purse, and shut the door behind her.

As she made her way down the street, the sun perched

itself upon a cloud, not yet sharing its light with the world. She could hear the familiar sound of the boat horns at the harbor, the seagulls squawking and flying above her. There were not many people out yet, but a few made their way into Mainsail's coffee shop. Charlotte followed. Coffee was essential at this point.

As she grabbed her iced coffee and turned around, a familiar face greeted her.

"Morning," Wes smiled.

"Good morning," Charlotte said, taking a sip of her coffee.

"Iced, good choice," he remarked, holding up his own cup. He must have been standing behind her.

"A must today," she joked, her throbbing headache welcoming the caffeine.

"Did you have fun last night?" he asked.

"I did, you *actually* have a lovely voice. Quite unexpected," she grinned.

"Oh well, I will take that as a compliment," he joked. "Off to work?"

"Yes, taking my time," she said, getting ready to walk towards the door.

"It was great seeing you again last night," he said, most sincerely.

Charlotte paused, her lips curling into a smile.

"You too," she said.

As she turned to leave, the joy in her eyes sparkled with the emerging sun outside. Wes was intriguing. She knew he already loved another, but the small hints he was trailing her with seemed to suggest something more. She knew he was probably just being friendly, after all, the whole town loved him. Last night, she caught a glimpse of the more laid-back version of him, a carefree soul that enjoyed his town's company. She felt he was strongly connected here, like the sailboats that called these waters home. People traveled back to Newport when the weather got warmer, and Charlotte could now see why. Its welcoming and gracious society was infectious.

"Good morning to you," Piper's cheery voice filled the shop as Charlotte walked in.

"Morning." She set her coffee on the counter. "Those margaritas were delish, but man, am I paying for it now," she said, rubbing her forehead.

"Take this," Piper offered an Excedrin.

"Thank you," Charlotte smiled.

As they worked, they playfully chatted about the evening, and not many guests had entered the store. Both were thankful for a slow day.

"Want to go out for lunch?" Piper asked, "We have a whole hour."

"Sure, I've wanted to try that place down the way by the pier," Charlotte confessed.

"Oh, umm, Dock's?" she asked.

"Yes, that's it!"

"Well, let's go then, it shouldn't be busy there yet."

The women grabbed an outside seat, placed directly above the water. The view was incomparable, the light breeze refreshing. They each ordered the customary lobster roll and a small cup of their New England clam chowder. Both creamy and delicious, they ate their food in silence for a few minutes before breaking into another conversation.

"So you didn't get a chance to tell me last night, who is Asher?"

Charlotte stopped chewing, looking off into the distance.

"I don't mean to pry. If it's too much, you don't have to tell me."

"No, it's just my ex-husband," she started to explain. "No secret there."

"Is he still in Seattle?"

"Yes, I left everything and came here. All I had with me was a single box. It just wasn't a good situation," she admitted.

"Was he...?" Piper prodded.

"Not at all," Charlotte answered her assumption. "He just wasn't very understanding of what I was going through at the time, he was very manipulative."

"Gotcha, well, your secrets are safe with me." Piper smiled. "My parents got divorced when I was in high school. It was terrible to witness, but when everything settled down, it was clear to see that it was the best decision. My mom and I got even closer, and for that I am thankful," she said, taking a drink of her iced water, her fingerprints leaving their mark on her sweating glass. "You really are brave, though, coming to an entirely new place, not knowing anybody."

"It was scary at first, but I can now say it's one of the best things I've ever decided to do. You don't really know how much you can go through until you do. I've learned a lot about myself."

"I bet," Piper smiled, "I'm glad you decided on

Newport."

"Me too," Charlotte agreed, taking a bite out of her lobster roll, the buttery bun made her mouth water. "What do you want to do? Are you going to stay here forever?"

Piper smiled and her eyes widened, "I would love to take over Finnegan's one day, if Debbie ever wanted to step down. I'm taking business classes online, trying to learn as much as I can."

"So when everyone went off to college, you stayed around here?"

"Yeah, college is expensive, and my parents just didn't have the means to pay for it. So, Finnegan's it is, as long as I work there," Piper said.

"That's smart," Charlotte said. "At least you'll graduate with no debt."

"At the time, it was really hard watching everyone leave and run off to different colleges. Everyone would ask where I was going, and I had to tell them I wasn't. I know my path will be longer than most, but I am determined to finish."

"You know, you're very wise," Charlotte said.

"Who, me?" she laughed.

"Trust me, that's a great quality for you to have. Take your time, there's no rush to grow up," Charlotte said.

The women devoured their food, laughing and talking as if they had been old friends for years. Piper had an easy, likable personality, and Charlotte was so thankful for her friendship.

"So, my dad has a sailboat docked over there," she pointed. "Would you like to go out and sail around the harbor with me?"

"Really? You know how to sail?" Charlotte asked.

"I grew up here, remember? You practically learn how to sail before you learn to ride a bike."

"I would love that."

The afternoon was breezy, but Charlotte welcomed it. As she steadily walked forward, she felt the pier teeter under her feet.

"It moves," Piper laughed.

"I can see that now," Charlotte said. Her hands extended a bit to keep her balance.

"You won't fall in," Piper assured her.

"I hope not!" Charlotte said, approaching the small sailboat. "Well, this is beautiful."

Piper extended a hand to help Charlotte down into the boat.

"It's not the biggest one in the world," Piper said. "But this is the one my dad taught me how to sail in. We've kept it ever since. He always tells me he could never sell it."

"That's really sweet," Charlotte said.

"See, it only has one sail," Piper said. "You can sit here while I get everything ready."

Charlotte took a seat in the cockpit as she watched Piper untie the boat from the dock to prepare for departure.

"So, how far out in the water are we going?" Charlotte asked.

"Not that far. I thought we'd piddle around the harbor a bit and talk," Piper said.

"I like that idea," Charlotte said. "Can I help with anything?"

"Not at all, just sit back and relax."

Charlotte sat back as she watched Piper flick on the motor.

"When does the sail go up?" Charlotte asked.

"Not until we get out there," Piper said.

As the boat inched forward, Charlotte sat back and traced the harbor with her eyes, taking in every detail. Other boats were parked in the harbor and anchored deep into the sand. Laughter and music danced past her ears as their boat passed others, people waving from a distance. Piper and Charlotte waved back, a silent understanding of the happiness of those lucky enough to enjoy the ocean at this vantage point. Charlotte turned her head to get a good look at the Wharf as they slowly made their way farther from shore. She made out Diego's, her favorite bar, perched above the others. Music from Dock's echoed in the breeze as the wind brushed salt against her skin.

"Just a little farther," Piper said.

Charlotte looked up and noticed the concentration on Piper's face. She could tell maneuvering this sailboat was ingrained in her soul. Every move she made was with purpose, ensuring their safety. She was the picture of quintessential Rhode Island with her white sweater draped and tied around her shoulders, keeping her warm. Her chino pants were cuffed at the bottom, and her dark leather Sperry boat shoes kept her steady.

Piper turned off the motor and checked the wind vane at the top of the mast to ensure they were moving towards the wind. She took her place on the deck, pulled on the halyard, and released the sail ties. She pulled the ties with much force, releasing the main sail. The beige sail puffed as the wind flapped its edges. The sail caught the breeze, and the boat lurched forward. Charlotte was amazed at how effortless Piper made it all seem.

"I thought we'd sail around a bit before stopping," she said, walking back towards Charlotte.

"Ok!" Charlotte said.

The water was glossy and calm, luminous to the eye. Charlotte inhaled a deep breath and closed her eyes as she exhaled, noticing a slight chill nip the edge of her nose. She tapped into her senses, allowing them to run free. The bow pointed up and down, riding between the white caps of the small waves, the sea creating its own symphony. It was its own maestro, trembling under its steady beat. The serenity was ruptured by the piercing cry of the gulls above, their language foreign to the human ear. She opened her eyes just as a white pelican dipped its bill beneath the ocean's surface, scooping up a small fish for lunch.

"Did you see that?" Piper gasped.

"Yes!" Charlotte exclaimed.

"You don't see that too often," Piper said.

Charlotte noticed a Victorian mansion surrounded by farmland off to the left, with a long pier that jutted out far into the water.

"What's that?" she pointed.

"Oh, that's the Kennedy's old house," Piper said.

Charlotte suddenly whipped her head back to face Piper, "As in...President Kennedy?"

"Well, actually, it was first the childhood home of Jackie Kennedy until she married John F. Kennedy."

"That's really cool," Charlotte said.

As they sailed, a large lawn filled with white Adirondack chairs came into view.

"And that?" Charlotte asked.

"Oh, that's Castle Hill Inn, I have to take you there for a drink sometime!" she said.

The large cream Inn sat atop a hill, its quaintness and beauty not lost on Charlotte.

As Piper turned the boat, its sides rocked back and forth, cradled by the water. She allowed the wind to propel them forward, back to Newport harbor. Once there, Piper stood up, released the sails, and slowed the boat to a halt. The sailboat bobbed upon the waves, the wind pressure successfully off the sails.

"I packed a little charcuterie board," Piper said. "Would you like a blanket, too? It can get chilly on the water."

"Yes, thank you."

Piper opened a latch, grabbed a few blankets, and tossed one to Charlotte. She wrapped it around herself before taking a seat across from her, who was opening up their chilled bottle of Pinot Grigio.

"I brought Solo Cups," Piper said. "Classy, I know."

"Honestly, that's perfect," Charlotte laughed.

They munched on their snacks and took sips of their wine as they chatted.

"I just want the house, the husband, and a gaggle of kids," Piper said.

Charlotte smiled, trying to hide her apprehension. She knew that was a normal dream to most, but felt jaded after her own experiences with the sought after "American Dream."

"Can I give you one piece of advice?" Charlotte asked.

"Of course," Piper said, plopping a green olive into her mouth.

"Get to know yourself really well first," she said.

Piper didn't say a word as she looked into Charlotte's eyes and crushed the olive with her molars. She could sense this sentiment was coming from experience.

"Do as much traveling as you can before having kids or getting married."

"I've always wanted to go to Europe," Piper said.

"Book the trip," she said, "because down the road, you don't want to regret never going."

Piper shifted in her seat, looking out at the ocean. Her eyes were longing for a glimpse of her future.

"I promise I'm not trying to make it seem so daunting, Lord knows I'm not the picture of a successful marriage, but I just wish someone had urged me more to follow my own passions, that's all."

"It makes sense," Piper said. "Where have you always wanted to go?"

"Now?" Charlotte asked as Piper nodded. "Edinburgh, Scotland."

"What's stopping you?"

Charlotte pondered her question.

"Fear."

"Of what?" Piper asked.

"Of not knowing anyone, being by myself. I mean, I won't even go to the movie theater alone."

"Yeah, but you came here all by yourself."

Piper was right. What *was* stopping her? She had just proven to herself she was more than capable of being alone and making it work, location not included.

"The only difference is a much longer plane ride," Piper laughed.

"Let me just get comfortable here first," Charlotte said.

"Well, you're already doing a good job of that."

Charlotte blushed and brushed off the compliment, something she had trained herself to do.

Piper suddenly pulled out her phone and pointed it at Charlotte. "Oh, the lighting is perfect, smile!" The iPhone flashed, and she turned her phone around to show her friend. "Now that's a good photo," Piper said.

Charlotte used to hate having her picture taken. She would always critique herself and point out her flaws. Yet in that moment, she paused, and her eyes started to well up.

"What's wrong?" Piper asked. "I can retake it!"

"No, no," Charlotte said. "I look so…happy."

Piper smiled and allowed her to soak in the moment. She extended her arm and caressed Charlotte's shoulder, offering support.

"I haven't seen myself smile like that in such a long time, Piper," she said. "Thank you."

She looked up at Piper, still holding the phone, as her misty eyes brightened.

"You deserve it," Piper said.

Chapter 8

Newport, Rhode Island, Present Day: Wes

The summer air danced through his lungs as he strolled through the harbor. He had the weekend off and was looking forward to having time to relax. June was fast approaching as May budded its final flowers. He loved Newport in the summer; it came alive, especially on concert nights. He loved how comforting it was for everyone in town to support him, and also just take a break from their busy lives to listen to him sing. It was never about him, though; he loved seeing people's faces relax as they settled into their seats among friends and family. It was something he was once so afraid of, but Emily, his fiancée, had encouraged it. He was grateful for her in that respect; she had led him towards the confidence he had today; however, her delivery could be abrasive, especially towards others.

"What are your plans for today?" Emily smiled, emerging from the corner store.

"Not sure," he said, holding onto his notebook. "I was thinking of going to the park or maybe taking a ride down Ocean Drive. Been working on a few lyrics for a new song," he explained.

"I love that," she shared, her hand meeting his.

"What about you?" he asked.

"I'm about to meet a friend up at Dock's for brunch. Are you sure you don't want company?" she asked.

"No, you do your own thing. I'll catch up with you after."

There was nothing better than a weekend, especially when you didn't have the pressures of work looming around you. As Emily lightly kissed his cheek and left his side, Wes walked back toward their condo to grab his car keys. He felt a drive towards the ocean would help ease the thoughts bouncing around his mind. The water seemed to calm him down in a way he could not really explain. The tide's changing pace matched the emotions in his mind. It seemed to bring peace to his anxiety, something that's been plaguing him for some time now. He couldn't pinpoint the direct cause of it, but knew it would reveal itself with time. For now, the ocean was his main form of therapy.

As his car glided down the historic Bellevue Avenue, he awaited the sights of the ocean. Bright red tulips were in full bloom, trailing the sidewalks. He noticed people walking their dogs and enjoying their day. Warmer weather brought out the best in people. As he took a turn at the end of the road, he could see the water behind the tall sea grass. The road unfolded into a dream, the blue water absorbing all the sunlight of the day, as if the waves were glazed with silk. He continued to drive until he found a spot that was less crowded. After a few minutes, he found the perfect place. He parked his car, grabbed his notebook, and shut his car door. He looked before him, scanning his surroundings. After a few moments, he walked across the road, took off his shoes, and walked a little further to where he saw a small patch of seagrass among the rocks. The waves were calm, soothing ripples breaking upon the shore. A few sailboats bobbed in the distance, slowly making their way to downtown.

As he concentrated on the lyrics spewing out onto the page in his journal, he could not ignore the image of Charlotte in his mind. He remembered her presence at the Wharf, her smile warming everyone around her. He knew it wasn't right to think about her when he was engaged, but it was something he seemed to not be able to escape. She was somewhat of a mystery to him. He had seen his grandmother talking with her as if they were old friends. He knew he needed to ask how they knew each other, but tabbed that into the back of his mind for now. He wondered if she truly enjoyed his music or if she was just being polite. He had hoped she enjoyed herself. The margaritas she was having showed a more relaxed side of her. He began to wonder why she had traveled to the East Coast alone. He often speculated *who* had driven such a sweet soul away. He felt instantly grateful because it caused her to drift to Rhode Island.

***

Newport, Rhode Island, Present Day: Charlotte

The farmers' market on Thames Street was becoming one of Charlotte's favorite spots. People grazed the small businesses ranging from flower shops, soaps, and candles, to food and other pleasantries. Susan strolled alongside her, marveling at the flower stand.

"You always need fresh flowers on your kitchen table," Susan remarked.

"Is that so?" Charlotte laughed.

"Yes, nothing cheers up guests more."

They stopped, Susan thumbing through the fresh bouquets, carefully inspecting them.

"What is your favorite flower, dear?" she asked.

"Well, I'm more of a tulip and hydrangea girl myself," she said, fingering the pink roses.

"We have plenty of those this season," the seller said, showing off a small bouquet of bright orange and deep pink tulips.

"I'll take those!" Charlotte gaped, "How much?"

"Ten dollars," he said.

Charlotte pulled out a ten-dollar bill and handed it to the gentleman. He handed her the bouquet with a smile.

"Those are beautiful," Susan said.

They continued on, Charlotte glancing down again at her tulips wrapped in light brown, delicate paper tied with a thin twine bow.

"So you had fun at the concert the other night," Susan said.

"I did," Charlotte said, assuming there was more to her statement. "It's so nice how everyone comes together."

"You've discovered Newport's charm," Susan said.

Silence filled the air between them as they took their seats outside the bakery, The Cookie Jar.

"Care for a treat?" Susan asked.

"I would love one," Charlotte said.

Moments later, Susan emerged from the shop with two large white chocolate lemon cookies.

"These are my absolute favorites," she said, handing one to Charlotte. "They are usually sold out by now, but we seem to have found some luck."

"Thank you."

They both enjoyed their cookies, laughing as they noticed all types of people enjoying the market. It was a beautiful sunny day. Charlotte's skirt swayed in the breeze as Susan perked up.

"I've been meaning to ask you this," she paused. "Why did you leave Seattle?"

People were starting to wonder why she had up and left her hometown, with nothing but a single box of her belongings. If she was being honest, she wasn't surprised.

"My divorce," Charlotte began.

"Oh, Susan, hello!" An abrupt, piercing tone cut through their conversation like a knife.

Susan rolled her eyes, already knowing who that voice belonged to. Charlotte sensed a jarring shift of energy at the unexpected interjection.

"Hi Emily," Susan mumbled. "Have you met my new friend, Charley?"

Charlotte's eyes brightened as she offered her hand to Emily to introduce herself. Emily glanced at Charlotte.

"Pleasure," she said, ignoring her introduction, and continued to chat with Susan. Charlotte's brows lifted in surprise as she nestled her hands back in her lap.

"I'll see you around," Emily said. "We still have lots to plan for the big day!"

Susan nodded as Emily walked away.

"She seems interesting," Charlotte said.

"Rude is what you meant to say," Susan replied. "Because she is."

Charlotte waved awkwardness away.

"So where were we?" Susan asked.

"I can't remember," Charlotte shrugged, welcoming the opportunity to conceal her secrets another day.

***

Several months later, Charlotte and Asher had met each other's friends and enjoyed small dates together here and there. Asher's schedule was very demanding, but the two made sure to make the best of it whenever he was in town.

"I just don't like him," Charlotte's friend, Kate, said, "he just isn't the one for you."

Kate had been Charlotte's first friend in Seattle. She was a waitress at the restaurant Charlotte worked at, and was her voice of reason. Although she was a bit younger than Charlotte, she was very wise beyond her years. They hung out almost daily, venting and sharing life's frustrations with each other. Kate was from New York with a feisty attitude to match. Charlotte was encouraged by her boldness, often relying on it to make decisions. It was usually easy for them to agree on something, until now.

"What?" Charlotte asked, genuinely surprised, not sure if the noisiness in the bar had muffled her friends' words.

"He's just so, I don't know, serious," she said, taking a swig of her Sauvignon Blanc.

"That's just how he is towards people he doesn't know very well," Charlotte stated, growing agitated.

Kate peered at Charlotte so intently, "Why are you getting defensive?" she noticed.

"I'm sorry, I'm just sick of explaining to people why I love him," Charlotte sighed.

"Well, there's the problem," Kate smiled.

Charlotte shrugged as she took a sip of her wine, looking out the window of the bar at people hurriedly walking by.

"I know you must love him," Kate said, "I'm not saying there is anything wrong with that. I just don't see it lasting long term."

That stung Charlotte's heart. The man she had been getting to know for the past six months was still not receiving her friends' approval. She knew that shouldn't be everything to her, but it did weigh negatively on her heart. She wanted her friends to enjoy her boyfriend. She wanted to be able to bring him out with her to have fun, but the feeling she was getting from her friend made her uncomfortable.

"Do you see it lasting long term?" Kate asked.

Charlotte turned to her, her eyes beginning to wet.

"I'm not trying to upset you," she said, grasping her hand from across the table.

"I know you're not," Charlotte said, "it's just so frustrating. You're not my first friend to say this."

Kate looked at Charlotte's eyes and grew empathetic. Charlotte wanted so desperately to be in love. She wanted that fairy tale ending, but Kate would not be able to live with herself if she never told her friend how she truly felt about Asher.

"Just have fun," Kate said, "keep it light."

***

Seattle, Washington, Two Years Prior

Charlotte headed out of work early to meet a friend for dinner. It had been a long day, but this dinner would offer her some respite. Work had been demanding lately. The owner of the restaurant, Mr. Duvale, was trying to expand their small space in Bainbridge Island to a bigger place in Seattle. Charlotte didn't feel it would be a better fit, but was finding it hard to convince him otherwise. She felt the excitement of the city might take away from the small-town charm his restaurant had.

Head to the sushi place in town, Rebecca had texted her earlier.

On my way, Charlotte responded.

Heading out of the parking lot, Charlotte turned on her favorite song, its lyrics sending her back in time.

As she approached the entrance of the restaurant, she was welcomed by the distinct aroma of warm white rice and tangy seasonings. She walked in to see Rebecca patiently waiting at a table by the window, looking through the menu. Her wavy brown hair hung just past her shoulders.

"Hey," Charlotte said, hugging her friend.

"Hey, how was your day?" Rebecca asked, returning a warm embrace.

"Busy. Duvale wants to expand the restaurant here in the city, and I just don't think it'll work," Charlotte rationalized.

"Really? Why not?" Rebecca asked, playing devil's advocate.

"It's just too small. If we tried to expand, I'd be afraid our client base couldn't keep up. More space means more money, and I'm not sure we could bring in enough," Charlotte explained, taking off her coat and settling into her seat. "Plus, I want it to keep its charm. The city might commercialize it."

"Sounds like you need a drink," Rebecca said, raising a brow.

"Oh, trust me—I *want* one," Charlotte admitted. "Like... several."

Rebecca laughed. "Rough week?"

"Rough month," Charlotte corrected. "I just feel stretched thin, like everything is on me all the time."

"How are *you* holding up?" Rebecca asked gently.

Charlotte shrugged. "Depends on the hour."

"I swear, you're so vague," Rebecca teased. "If it were me, I'd be spiraling."

"Good thing it's not you then," Charlotte smiled.

"Is Asher any better? Helping at all?"

"He does...sometimes," Charlotte said, knowing it wasn't entirely true. "I get irritated easily, but it's probably just stress."

Rebecca gave her a look. "Are you *sure* about that?"

Rebecca wasn't naive. She'd known Asher since they were teenagers. She knew how arrogant he could be, but she also knew how compassionate he could be—it was a double-edged sword. Charlotte often wondered if the two had ever shared feelings for each other, but they both denied any trace of attraction.

After dinner, Charlotte made her way back home, and she noticed the kitchen light on.

As she walked in, Asher was making dinner, a bottle of wine open.

"How was your day?" he smiled, taking a swig of the ruby red bordeaux.

"Busy," she reiterated.

"Have a seat, you earned it," he enticed her, pulling out a chair for her at the kitchen island.

Charlotte hesitantly climbed into the chair, her eyes flicking to the wine and then back to Asher. She was careful with her words; she didn't want to disrupt the rare calm that the wine seemed to have brought him.

"I'm sorry for how I've acted recently," he said quietly. "I know I haven't made things easy for you."

Charlotte blinked, caught off guard as he continued.

"I haven't been the most patient person toward you. I see that now," he admitted. "I made dinner, but I think you already ate with Rebecca."

"I did—but now I've got lunch for tomorrow," Charlotte said with a small smile.

"How was dinner…with Rebecca?" he asked, a hint of hesitation in his voice.

"It was good, the sushi was on point as usual."

"Oh, you went to Chang's?"

"Yes, it was sushi night, half off rolls," she continued.

"What did you guys talk about?"

"Work, life, husbands…"

Asher's attention perked up.

"Don't worry, we didn't talk about you," Charlotte insisted, covering her lie.

"I'm sure," he laughed. "Something going on between Rebecca and Luke?"

"Just the same old stuff, you know," she said.

"I thought they were in therapy?" Asher inquired.

"They were, but not sure anymore. She mentioned it wasn't helping much."

"Oh, I see," he muttered, finishing his wine glass suddenly.

Chapter 9

"Funny to see you here, dear," Susan smiled, surprised to see her grandson on her front steps.

"What? I can't drop in to say hello to my favorite grandmother?" he joked.

The soft rustle of the brown grocery bags filled the pantry as Charlotte placed their farmers market goodies away onto the shelves. Jars of sweet pickles and tomatoes were just a few things Susan couldn't leave without buying. She paused, hearing the rhythmic sound of movement coming into the kitchen and the low hum of the refrigerator.

"You truly think you are funny, don't you?" she laughed.

Charlotte's breath caught as she mistakenly released a jar of pickles from her hands. Her pulse quickened, and a surge of adrenaline flooded her veins. She didn't move, she didn't blink, as if her stillness might keep her from being noticed.

She recognized that voice.

"What was that?" the voice gasped. His footsteps grew louder and louder towards the pantry door. It flung open before she could move.

"Wait, Charley?" Wes exclaimed, bewildered by her

sudden presence in his grandmother's kitchen.

"You two know each other?" Susan appeared next to him, her eyebrows furrowed.

"Well, we've met a few times," he said.

Charlotte stood frozen in the pantry, barricaded by both Susan and Wes. Her eyes darted between them.

"Lovely," Susan said. "Then you've met my new roommate," she said to Wes.

"What?" Wes asked, his arms now folded in front of his chest.

"She needed a place to stay, so I offered her a room until she gets back on her feet. Anyway, you got off work early today," she said, looking at the old clock above her kitchen table and clearly trying to change the subject.

"Didn't have to work today, actually. Just came from Ocean Drive," he explained.

"Can I...just get past you?" Charlotte asked, slithering by him.

"Oh, of course, sorry," he said. The initial shock wearing off.

"How did you guys meet?" Wes asked.

"Well, it's pretty simple," Susan explained. "She was homeless and needed a place to stay."

Charlotte whipped her head around. "I wasn't homeless, I was staying at the hotel up the road."

"So you took in a stray?" Wes laughed.

Charlotte rolled her eyes.

"Kind of," Susan laughed.

"You two are impossible," Charlotte said.

"Welcome to the family," Wes said. "I always wanted

a sister."

Susan smacked Wes on the shoulder as he opened the refrigerator door.

"I need a beer," he laughed. "Wait, you're not here to ransack my grandmother's house, are you?"

Charlotte peered at him, "No, I would never do such a thing!"

"He's kidding, dear," Susan smiled.

Charlotte huffed as she took a seat at the table.

Wes grabbed his drink and plopped into the seat across from her.

"I finished putting away the groceries," Charlotte said to Susan.

"Thank you," she said. "You didn't have to do all of that."

"I wanted to," Charlotte said. "But you lost a jar of pickles."

"Homeless and clumsy," Wes laughed.

"Impossible," Charlotte repeated.

Susan glanced at her grandson, "Before this marvelous introduction, you looked like something was on your mind."

"Kind of, I guess," he admitted.

She could see his eyebrows slightly curving in as he looked out the window. His usually calm expressions seemed strained; he was harboring something in that mind of his, and she wanted to help.

"How's Emily?" she incited, hoping this might spark conversation and bring the problem to its head.

Wes took a minute to answer, a large sigh billowed from his chest.

"She's fine," he started. "I just feel so anxious lately, I'm not even sure why."

He crossed his hands in front of him, his robust shoulders curving inward.

"Maybe it's just wedding jitters," Susan offered. "It's a big deal planning a wedding."

"No, it's not that," he said. "I've barely helped with it; I've been working so much."

"Having cold feet then?" Susan questioned.

Charlotte stared at the floor. She felt like she shouldn't be included in such an intimate conversation.

Wes stopped and stared at his grandmother. If there was anyone in the world who knew him, it was her. He could see her concerned eyes staring back at him, a world of experiences, she was not naive when it came to relationships.

"I'm not sure," he confided."I love Emily, I've loved her for many years, but..."

"You're bored," Susan declared.

Charlotte's cheeks grew rosy at Susan's abruptness.

Wes shrugged his shoulders; he wasn't even sure *that* was it. Something was off, but he could not pinpoint it. Bored would be fine. Bored was natural when you'd been with someone for so long. A problem like that could be easily fixed by finding a new hobby or encouraging a way to ignite the spark. The emotions he felt ran deeper, and he couldn't tell if it was natural to feel this way anymore.

"It's okay," Susan comforted. "Whatever it is, it will unveil itself to you when it's supposed to."

"Hope so," Wes replied.

"All in good time," she said.

After a few silent moments between them, Susan changed the subject. She could tell her grandson was struggling with something, but she didn't want to poke too much, especially in front of Charlotte. She wanted him to come to her, like he had so many times before. His company meant the world to her, and she wanted to help in anyway she could. After all, she knew her time on this earth was limited. Getting older puts a lot of things into perspective. Family always came first.

"So Seattle," Wes sarcastically nicknamed Charlotte. "What are you doing tonight?"

***

Seattle, Washington, Two Years Prior

It was a calm Saturday morning, the living room was dimly lit; the warm glow from the lamp cast long shadows against the wall. The coffee pot was slowly brewing, the sunshine barely peeking around the gray clouds. Charlotte put on her slippers, grabbed her bathrobe, and glided down the hall to the kitchen. The coffee pot sputtered for a bit, signaling its brewing was complete. Asher was at his desk near the large bay window, his back towards her. His headphones were on; she figured he was listening to music as he worked. He often liked to do a few things over the weekend to make the week ahead easier. She decided she would surprise him with a hug, but before she did, something on the computer screen caught her eye, and she paused. It was an email chain, with the name *Rebecca* on most of them. She tried to look closely when Asher's chair suddenly spun around as he quickly closed his laptop, his eyes darting to the window, avoiding hers.

"Good morning," he said, standing up. His jaw tightened, and the air between them thickened with tension.

"Are you emailing Rebecca?" Charlotte asked again.

"You're overreacting," he said, wiping his palms on his jeans before turning toward her. "She asked if I knew a couple's therapist. You know, for her and Luke," he sputtered.

"You? You know therapists?" she asked as her eyebrows rose, unconvinced.

"Yeah, I have a friend in the city who does couples therapy. A guy from college," he said. "Would you like some coffee?" he asked, changing the subject.

"I'd like you to be honest with me," Charlotte said.

"I don't know what you expect from me, Charlotte. I'm not hiding anything," he said as his posture stiffened, walking over to the counter.

"Because something's off," she said. "I can feel it, I have felt it for a while, you've been distant lately."

Asher's lips thinned, "You're making this into something it's not."

Charlotte could feel a knot tightening in her stomach, her breath becoming shallow.

"You can't even look me in the eyes," she said.

Asher shifted uncomfortably, still avoiding her stare.

"I don't know why you're making this about her. I'm just doing the right thing and suggesting a therapist to a friend," he said.

Charlotte's heart dropped; she had heard similar defenses before. The same empty words spewing from his mouth, trying to convince her she was the crazy one. Charlotte realized then what he was doing: he was trying to turn *her* into the villain. With a shaky breath, she turned to leave, knowing she wasn't going to get what she wanted out of this conversation. The truth was already slipping through the cracks, and she had seen it clear as day on his computer screen.

***

Newport, Rhode Island, Present Day: Charlotte & Wes

"Charley!" a voice shouted from a distance as Charlotte and Wes walked into the Wharf.

"Hey Piper," Charlotte smiled.

"Do you guys work together?" Wes asked.

"Yes we do," Piper replied, giving both of them a hug hello. "How do you know Wes?"

"My grandmother picked up a stray," he laughed.

Charlotte's head tilted as she frowned at him. "She offered me a room; it was very generous of her."

"And Emily's okay with that?" Piper turned to Wes.

"It wasn't my idea," Wes shrugged.

Charlotte's back stiffened.

"Wes!" a high-pitched voice called out.

As Piper turned, Emily's figure emerged from the entrance at Dock's.

"Hey," Wes said, waving her over. "Have you met Charlotte?"

Emily's smile quickly flattened as she turned her nose up, "Briefly," she said.

"It's nice to see you again," Charlotte said, this time keeping her hands at her sides.

Piper locked arms with Charlotte as she said, "Let's go

in so I can introduce you to our small circle of friends."

Charlotte nodded as Piper quickly shuffled her into the bar.

"I think I'm understanding why she is not everyone's favorite person," Charlotte said.

"Good," Piper said. "She's not a good fit for Wes either; we all see it."

As they walked up to the bar and placed their bags on their seats, Piper began introducing Charlotte to their group of friends while simultaneously ordering them a drink. The bar was alive with energy, clinking glasses and conversations blended like a symphony. It was pretty packed, many people who couldn't find a seat were hovering nearby; luckily, Piper's friends kept a few seats open for them. Behind the bar, the row taps were in full swing, the bartender's hands a blur as they crafted cocktails and poured beers into icy glasses.

"Everyone," Piper announced. "This is my friend Charlotte."

A few of the guys exchanged glances, their eyes lingering on Charlotte a little longer than necessary.

"We've heard there was a new girl," Paul said. "I'm Paul," as he extended his hand, his handshake firm.

"Nice to meet you," Charlotte said.

Paul nudged his friend, Ryan, who was sitting next to him.

"Hello," Ryan said with a kind smile.

Charlotte forced a smile, feeling her cheeks warm. She glanced around and noticed Emily and Wes in the corner of her eye, ordering their drinks at the other end of the bar. She could feel Wes's presence, even though he wasn't speaking directly to her. His eyes flickered to Charlotte as Emily began a conversation with another friend, his gaze catching her on fire. She noticed the tightening in his jaw, something deeper forming in his eyes. It was a slight admission of longing, as if he were somewhere else with her, for a brief moment. Charlotte's breath caught in her throat as her pulse quickened, her mind trying to make sense of it. Was it possible?

"Here you go," Piper said, handing Charlotte a glass of wine.

Charlotte quickly took a sip, pretending to focus on her drink. Emily was blissfully unaware as her head fell back in laughter at someone else's joke. Wes's attention kept slipping back to Charlotte, his lips parted slightly, as if he were to speak. Charlotte's stomach twisted as Paul approached her.

"So, Seattle, how are you liking things on the East Coast?"

"You're in on the nickname, too?" she grinned.

"Wes said it a few times, and it just stuck," he said.

"I like it a lot," she said. "I'm so glad I came here."

As Paul went on about his job at the marina, Charlotte's gaze betrayed her as she looked back at Wes. Her hands tightened around her glass as she caught his soft stare, almost regretful. The air was palpable now, an unspoken question hanging between them.

"Let's go outside and grab a table," Piper suggested to the group.

All eight of them agreed, grabbed their drinks, and headed for one of the tables outside overlooking the ocean. The sun cast a golden hue on the horizon as a few boats bobbed in the harbor.

"So, you came all the way from Seattle?" One of their friends asked.

"Yes," Charlotte answered.

"How did you settle on Newport?" Another asked.

"Well, my grandparents lived here and I used to vacation here a lot in the summer as a kid," she started to explain.

"I heard you were going through a nasty divorce," Emily shouted out from the other end of the table.

Charlotte's cheeks instantly caught fire as everyone's heads spun to her. She looked away and then raised her eyes to Emily. Emily sat stoic as she took a sip of her drink, her eyes confidently staring back. Charlotte hadn't told anyone why she had fled. How did she know?

"Well, I..." Charlotte began to explain.

"It's not any of our business," Piper interrupted.

Wes's jaw tensed as he shifted in his seat, mumbling something to Emily. She couldn't hear what was said, but Emily's eyes rolled to the back of her head in response.

"Anyone going to Boston for the game next week?" someone asked, changing the subject.

As a new conversation blossomed among old friends, Charlotte couldn't help but feel out of place. She sank back into her seat, trying not to make eye contact with anyone. Old feelings of insecurity that she had laid to rest suddenly began aching in her chest. She took a deep breath and a few sips of her drink to ease her embarrassment.

"We can go," Piper whispered.

"No, it's alright," Charlotte said. "I'm going to get another drink at the bar. Would you like another?"

"Sure," Piper smiled.

Charlotte shuffled over to the bar as quickly as she could, placing their drink order with the bartender. Nobody at the table questioned where she was going. As she waited, she tapped her fingers along the wooden table as if to channel her anxious thoughts.

"I'm sorry about her," Wes said, placing his hand on the small of her back.

Charlotte's spine straightened as his warmth radiated through her sweater.

"It's fine," Charlotte said, trying not to make eye contact.

"It's not," he said. "That's none of her business."

"She's right," Charlotte said. "Among other reasons."

Wes glanced down.

"I think I'm going to head home, anyway," she said. "Thank you for inviting me."

"What about your drinks?" he asked as they arrived.

"One's for Piper, but you can have mine. You may need it more than me."

His lips curled into a lopsided smirk as he paused as if deciding whether to respond. Instead, he let out a soft chuckle, a sign he understood her sarcasm completely.

"Good night," she said.

Charlotte walked alone along the cobblestone streets, her footsteps uneven on the worn stones. The soft glow of the antique streetlights flickered against the dark waves of the ocean, where wooden masts swayed gently in the breeze. A single tear rolled down her cheek, tracing a cold path to the edge of her chin. With her shoulders drawn tight, she headed back home.

Home.

***

Seattle, Washington, Two Years Prior

"Charlotte, are you ready?" Asher asked, yelling up the stairs.

"One more minute!" she shouted back.

She took one last look at herself in the full-length mirror and adjusted the straps on her shoulders for the third time. The dress clung to her curves tighter than anything she'd ever worn. The plunging neckline left little to the imagination, and the cherry red fabric was the brightest thing in her closet. The slit up her thigh felt daring, her own reflection foreign.

"Do I look alright?" she asked Asher as she slowly walked down the stairs.

"Is that the dress I picked out?" he gasped. "You look amazing."

The warmth of his stare felt genuine, something she hadn't seen in a while.

"Seriously, you look incredible," he said, brushing her arm as he circled behind her.

Charlotte forced a smile, trying to let the compliment land, but couldn't shake the feeling of discomfort.

"Let's get going," he said. "We don't want to leave Rebecca and Luke waiting."

The memory of Asher and Rebecca's strange email chain returned to the forefront of her mind. Whatever was happening between them would be revealed tonight; she would make sure of it.

As they made their way to the car, a chill in the air caused the hairs on Charlotte's neck to raise a little. It was the beginning of fall, leaves lay lifeless on the ground, bringing a certain dreariness to the Island. Fog began to settle on the street as they pulled out onto the main road. Charlotte's attitude matched the weather, gloomy and bleak.

"I haven't seen Luke in a while," Asher said.

"Me neither," Charlotte replied.

"Hopefully they don't argue tonight," he said, turning into the restaurant.

"That would be something," Charlotte smirked. She hated it when he acted like they were any better. Perhaps they needed therapy, too. Apparently, he knew a guy in the city.

"I'll get your door," he said, parking the car and quickly getting out.

Once inside, they settled at their table. Asher ordered a cocktail, and Charlotte ordered red wine.

"Hi!" Asher radiated once Rebecca and Luke walked in.

Charlotte smiled and slowly got up to give them both a hug.

"Been a while," Asher said to Luke, extending his right hand.

"Thanks for coming out," Rebecca smiled, hugging Asher. His hand lingered on the small of her back a little too long for Charlotte's liking.

"Always a pleasure," Asher whispered into her ear.

Charlotte's jaw tightened. Her blood started to slowly come to a boil beneath her skin.

As each couple took their seats, Charlotte noticed

Rebecca chose to sit farthest from her but directly across from Asher. Once seated, Rebecca looked up at him and smiled, raising the menu from her plate.

"So what do you all normally get?" she asked.

"I love the lasagna," Charlotte said. She wanted her to know she was paying attention.

"That sounds delicious," Rebecca replied, unfazed.

"I'm not a huge fan of pasta," Luke said.

Nobody responded.

"The manicotti always turns out great," Asher said, adding to the conversation.

"Yes, manicotti is another good one," Rebecca agreed.

Charlotte rolled her eyes. It would be a miracle if she did not blow up tonight.

The waitress walked over and got the rest of their drink orders. Rebecca ordered a Chardonnay, while Luke ordered a Bourbon.

The conversation seemed light and flowed easily among the couples once everyone got settled. After all, they had all been friends as couples for over five years. Charlotte's instincts pinged every so often. Either a glance or a smile from Rebecca to Asher made her stomach cringe.

"How's work, Asher?" Rebecca asked exclusively to him.

As Asher dove into answering her question, Charlotte noticed Rebecca's intense eye contact with her husband. When Asher spoke, her lips puckered, enhancing her dark maroon lipstick. Luke was oblivious, constantly checking something on his cell phone. The rest of the restaurant quietly buzzed with business, nothing out of the ordinary for a Sunday

night. Charlotte brought her glass to her lips as she noticed
Asher's exuberant replies to Rebecca's simple responses. He
was never *this* attentive to Charlotte. It caused her sadness,
but was quickly followed by rage. Her ears began to ring,
drowning out her inhibitions. Her clammy hands folded, her
heart leaping out of her chest.

"What are you two emailing each other about?"
Charlotte demanded.

Rebecca and Asher stopped talking to stare at her and
then back at each other. Both speechless. Luke looked up from
his phone; his fingers ceased typing.

"What?" Asher uttered.

"Yesterday morning, I saw a long email chain between
the two of you," Charlotte asserted.

Rebecca froze, not saying a word, her eyes fixed on
Asher. Asher grew increasingly annoyed, turning his body
towards his wife, his eyes blinking in disbelief.

"I told you, honey, she was asking for a therapist
recommendation."

He stilled, not turning to look at Rebecca. His calmness
unnerved her.

"That takes *one* email," Charlotte retorted. "Not as
many as I saw."

"Therapist?" Luke chimed in.

"Umm, yes, I don't like the one I currently have,"
Rebecca finally muttered, her voice shallow with deceit.

"For just you? I thought it was for *couples* therapy?"
Charlotte asked, staring into Asher's eyes, unveiling his lie.

"Couples therapy?" Luke asked again, "I'm confused."

"Our spouses are—" Charlotte started to say.

"I think you've said enough tonight," Asher said, his fist hitting the table, all four water glasses clanging against their respective silverware.

The table grew silent, and nobody made eye contact. Charlotte couldn't take the silence and arose from her chair, making her way to the bathroom. Her heart now thumping in her throat, she threw open the ladies' room door. She placed both hands on either side of the white sink, trying to catch her breath. She knew her husband could be sneaky, but to lie so outright? It crumbled the last bit of faith she had in him until it was like her heart fully broke. She did not expect it. After a few moments, she felt her lunch creep up her throat, the sudden urge to expel from her body. She ran to an open stall, locking the door behind her. Her stomach wretched as hot tears rolled down her cheeks.

"Charlotte?" A whisper from outside her stall emerged.

Charlotte ignored it, wiping her cheek with a small piece of toilet paper. She opened the stall door to see Rebecca standing there. Her solemn expression made Charlotte more queasy.

"Are you okay?" Rebecca repeated.

"Not necessarily," Charlotte said.

"I'm sorry. I promise nothing is going on; we are honestly just friends. I don't know why—" she continued until Charlotte stopped her.

"It just seems too obvious, his hand on your back," Charlotte said.

"What?" Rebecca asked, playing dumb.

"Nothing," Charlotte whispered.

"I have no reason to lie to you," Rebecca said, her

hands folded across her chest, her eyes looking down.

"I know," Charlotte said. She suddenly felt terrible. She felt she was making something out of nothing. They all thought she was losing her mind. Maybe it *was* in her mind? Regardless, she felt conflicted. She was friends with Rebecca but wouldn't necessarily label her more than that. Charlotte paused to wash her hands, watching Rebecca's expression behind her in the mirror. Charlotte's eyes narrowed in on her burgundy lipstick. She froze. She had seen that color before, but on who? Her mind flicked back to her and Asher's first date at the restaurant. She looked down at her own dress, the same bold red as the one that woman was wearing.

The mysterious woman from Asher's past.

How had she not pieced that together before now? Rebecca was Asher's ex-girlfriend.

As Charlotte lathered her fingers in warm water and soap, she glanced in the mirror and stopped. Her sunken and saddened eyes paralyzed her. She had suddenly remembered simpler times and longed for how it used to be. She felt a wave of nausea return in response to her newest realization, but waved it away.

She knew what she had to do next.

Find that email chain.

***

Charlotte glanced at the clock, her pupils shrinking as her eyes squinted to see the numbers more clearly.8:00 pm

She sighed as she carefully placed a small stack of paperwork in a neat pile in the center of her desk. She wanted to be able to remind herself what she needed to work on after the long Memorial Day weekend. She had no big plans; she and Asher discussed staying in and enjoying romantic dinners alone. It was hard enough to get alone time with both of their busy work schedules. Charlotte had been asked by a few friends to accompany them on an out of town trip, but she turned it down.

She flicked her desk light off as she grabbed her purse to head out the door. The restaurant was still packed, a buzz of chatter and the scratching of silverware on porcelain plates filled her ears as she got up to head out. As she closed and locked her office door, she glanced down the narrow hallway and noticed many patrons enjoying drinks at the bar; a few scattered occupied tables were still enjoying their meals as she zig-zagged through them. It was a holiday weekend, after all. She waved goodbye to a few colleagues as she exited, feeling the cool evening air swipe across her cheeks. The rain had stopped, but the street glistened under the lights, standing tall beside them. Her car was nestled in the corner lot, away from the guest parking. She had learned fairly quickly that when busy, it was difficult to leave.

Her heels clicked against the dark ocean of concrete as she walked to her car, checking her phone for text messages and missed calls. She noticed a one-line text message from Asher:

Hurry home, love.

Her chest pinched together as her lips curled into a smile, happiness brewing deep inside her heart.

Leaving now, see you soon.

When she arrived at her apartment, to which Asher had a key to, she noticed her kitchen lights were on. Once parked, she quickly grabbed her things and threw her car door shut. Her feet ached as she trudged up the stairs; the stress from a long day weighed her down. She was excited to change into comfy clothes and curl up on the couch. Once on the second floor, she placed her key card up to her *front door, and the light beside it turned green. As she walked, her eyes followed a trail of rose petals to the kitchen. Once there, Asher was standing beside the island, smiling from ear to ear.*

"What is all this?" Charlotte beamed. Asher handed her a glass of chilled Vieux Clicquot, her favorite, and an envelope.

"Open it," he said.

She placed her champagne glass on the counter as her fingers fervently peeled it open like a present. Charlotte slid the card out and opened it. Her eyes grew as wide as the sea when her brain had caught up to what Asher had done.

"Tonight," he said.

"What?" Charlotte asked.

"We're leaving tonight, in two hours. We're taking the red eye to Kiawah Island."

"South Carolina?" she asked.

"Yes!" Asher said.

He had secretly planned a holiday weekend getaway without her noticing at all. She was stunned. She bounced as she wrapped her arms around his neck, planting a kiss on his cheek. His hands rested on her hips as his chin dipped to allow his lips to meet hers.

She pulled away, "How long do I have to pack?"

Asher glanced down at his watch, "15 minutes. The limo is coming to take us to the airport in about 20 minutes."

Charlotte bolted to her bedroom and yanked her suitcase from her closet. She thumbed through her hangers, pausing to glance at certain blouses and dresses that caught her eye. She packed what she felt most confident in and threw her makeup bag inside before zipping her suitcase shut. She grabbed her hairbrush and gently ran it through her hair, her smile catching her attention in the bathroom mirror. Her giddiness felt childlike, a feeling that had not touched her soul in what had felt like a lifetime.

"Ready!" she exclaimed. Charlotte walked out back into the kitchen, her suitcase rolling behind her. Asher was thumbing through his phone, waiting for her, right where she had left him. A sliver of a smile crept onto his face as he saw her again, confirming he had successfully surprised her.

"Let's go," he said. Asher hoisted his duffel bag over his shoulder, making his way toward the door.

"Hold on," Charlotte said. She leaned back and turned her champagne glass up towards the sky, its bubbles tingling on her tongue as it made its way down to her stomach, "We can't let Vieux go to waste!"

Asher let out a laugh as he held the door for her, and she giggled as she walked out the door. Once outside, the shiny charcoal limo pulled up to her complex. A man dressed in all black opened his door and met them on the sidewalk. "Airport, sir?"

"Yes," Asher said.

"Of course, sir. Ma'am, allow me?" as he opened the trunk and gently slid her suitcase and Asher's Jackon's duffel bag inside. Once he shut the trunk, he rounded the corner and opened the door for them. Charlotte's cheeks blushed as she stepped in. She felt a little embarrassed at the regality of the moment. It wasn't often she felt like royalty. Once inside, the supple leather kissed her legs as she slid to the end of the seat, making room for Asher.

"My name is Edmond. If you need anything, just hit the button on the door, and it will alert me. My GPS says our estimated arrival time at the airport is 20 minutes. Please sit back and relax. Sir, the champagne you requested is chilling in an ice bucket to your right."His privacy window slowly slid up as quickly as it had slid down.

They were alone.

"What is all of this?" she asked.

Asher poured her another glass of champagne, this time one she could enjoy.

"It's all for you, my love," he said. They clinked their glasses together in a celebratory fashion, kissing each other to signify the start of their vacation.

As the limo sprang forward, Charlotte sat back and took another sip of her bubbly. A smile was plastered on her cheeks as she watched them merge onto the highway. She couldn't help but feel as if maybe this was it. Maybe this was when he would propose. He was romantic, she had learned, but their usual dates looked nothing like this. This had to be a special occasion. Her eyes darted to his pockets to search for a small square indent in his work pants, but she didn't find one.

It was probably in his bag, she figured.

The limo dropped them off at the carport, and they swiftly made their way inside. The security line, to their surprise, wasn't badly backed up. Once through, Asher checked their tickets and wheeled Charlotte's suitcase for her; his bag rested on top.

"Thank you," she smiled.

"Of course," he said.

When they arrived at their terminal, Asher suggested they sit at the bar for a drink. They had one hour to kill, after all. Charlotte asked countless details of their trip, and Asher refused to answer any of them, "I know it's unlike you to not plan and be surprised, but I want you to enjoy this." Asher ordered them both a drink and an appetizer to share.

"Well, nobody has ever surprised me like this," she said.

"You deserve it. You've been working like crazy lately, and

we both deserve to get away for a bit."

"Do I need to take Tuesday off?" she asked. "I don't want to worry about our plane being delayed or anything."

"No, we are flying out Monday morning. You'll have plenty of time to unpack and get ready for the week," he assured her.

Charlotte felt a wave of peace flow through her body. It was clear he understood her anxieties and anticipated her next thought with careful consideration. For her to relax and fully take advantage of their time off, he knew he had to take care of what would pester her like a gnat if he did not.

"Thank you," she said.

That next hour was filled with bouts of laughter and conversation. They discussed both work and personal goals. Asher listened intently, commenting between her thoughts, instilling a sense of confidence in her dreams. The way he rested his hand on her knee excited her. Whenever she made a good point, he would grip it a little tighter before pulling away. She yearned for more.

"We're boarding," he noticed.

He set his card on the bar and paid for their tab. Charlotte shuffled off the barstool and straightened her blouse, instantly regretting not changing into something more comfortable.

"We board first," Asher said.

"Really?" Charlotte asked. Charlotte glanced down at her ticket and saw the fine print in the right-hand corner under her terminal number. "First class?" she asked.

Asher winked and continued to walk to the ticket stand, Charlotte following closely behind.

Chapter 10

Newport, Rhode Island, Present Day: Wes & Charlotte

Wes decided to join some of his buddies at Diego's for a round of drinks. Saturday nights at the harbor were fun, something he didn't get to enjoy very often. Work had been extremely busy lately, and his mind had been filled with doubts. Emily was in Martha's Vineyard for a work trip, and Wes didn't feel like bumming it alone at home.

"Hey man, you made it!" Ryan smiled, lightly patting Wes on the back.

"Figured someone needed to keep an eye on you guys," Wes said, walking over to the bar.

"Can I get you anything?" the waiter asked, leaning forward toward them.

"Bud Light," Wes responded, "thanks, Felix."

"How have you been?" Wes's other friend, Paul, asked.

"Busy," Wes explained, rubbing two fingers down the bridge of his nose. "Both the hospital and office seem to always be packed lately."

"Well, there will always be sick people," Ryan chimed in.

"True," Wes said, glancing around the room. If he was being honest, he had hoped to find a familiar set of eyes. Instead, a small window was open, giving a slight view of the vast harbor. He saw a few sailboats docked, some for sightseeing purposes. His eyes focused on a sailboat preparing for a tour, its deckhands working furiously to prepare for their jaunt around the harbor. It was the perfect night for it, Wes thought. He watched as the deckhands checked for leaks in the hull and that the fuel tank was full. He noticed how they took special consideration, making sure the seacocks and thru-hulls were working properly. He yearned to be on a sailboat; after all, he had practically grown up on one. After retiring from medicine, his father owned a sailing business where touring companies rented out his sailboats. He offered it to Wes, but he declined. If only he had said what this heart had whispered, instead of what fear had commanded. He loved medicine and, more than anything, wanted to prove to his father that he could do it too. However, when the world went quiet, the truth lay thick in the air.

The Wharf was slowly coming to life. The hum of conversation filled the air as patrons devoured street tacos while watching the sunset slowly fall below the water's edge before them. It was something Wes often felt he took for granted. Working as much as he did, it was easy to forget how beautiful his hometown truly was.

"How's wedding planning?" Paul asked.

Wes took a swig of his beer, his jawline stiffening.

"It's going," he replied.

"I can't imagine everything that goes into planning an event like that," Ryan said.

"Yeah, and Emily's parents are pretty important around here," Paul said.

"Since her dad's the governor, hopefully he picks up

most of the bill, am I right?" Paul laughed.

Wes ignored his high school buddies' jokes. This wedding would be an important event for the town, for sure. His future father-in-law *was* a prominent figure in this community, so his expectations of the event and for Wes were pretty high. He remembered the night Emily casually discussed the number of people who had already rsvp'd. To Wes, the number was astronomical, but to Emily and her family, it was expected.

Wes pulled at his collar at the memory, a brief release.

"Another round!" Paul alerted their favorite bartender.

"What are we thinking?" Felix asked, placing his elbow on the counter, his eyes looking back at the large selection of liquor.

"Tequila," Paul said. "Anyone else in?"

Their nods to Felix signaled their allowance of the matter.

"What type?" Felix asked. "My favorite is the Corraleja, you can't go wrong."

"We trust you," Wes said.

"It is kind of pricey, you sure?" Felix asked.

"My man's a doctor," Paul said, slamming his hand on Wes's shoulder. "We can afford it."

"We?" Wes laughed.

"Yeah, we're family," Paul said.

Wes then noticed a few people enter the bar, and they caught his eye immediately. Charlotte walked in first, like a sailboat gliding into port. The three women behind her were smiling and searching for an open table or place at the bar. Charlotte's hair was loose, a book tucked beneath her arm, and a timid smile on her face that signaled she had been dragged there. They snagged the last four seats at the end of the bar, overlooking the water. He couldn't help but notice her. For someone who hadn't been in town all that long, she had certainly made herself known. She chatted with the other women, a shy smile brushing across her face as she lifted the cocktail menu. She lightly swept away her hair, exposing the nape of her neck, the wind gently drifting the rest behind her back. The slight chill of the breeze alerted Charlotte to pull her denim jacket up to hug her shoulders.

He could tell by her flushed cheeks that she didn't know everyone she was with, probably only Piper. Wes had gone through grade school with Piper. She was known to all as a nice person, someone who would welcome a newcomer with open arms. He knew both women worked with each other at Finnegan's, so he was not surprised a friendship would arise between them.

"I wish I had dated Piper," Ryan sighed. "When I had the chance."

Wes stayed silent, glancing back over at his friends.

"You had a chance? When?" Wes pestered.

"Remember? Sophomore year, and then that new kid flew in and snagged her," Ryan reminisced.

"You just dragged your feet for too long," Wes added.

"Probably so," Ryan admitted.

"I think she's single now," Paul said. "Why don't you send over a few tequila shots?"

"You think?" Ryan asked, straightening his back and tugging on the ends of his shirt.

"Yeah, why not?" Paul said. "It would give you a

reason to go over there."

Ryan turned towards the bar and ordered a round of tequila shots for the women as well. Wes grew interested; maybe this would give him time to speak with Charlotte alone, without the fear of his fiancée making it awkward. Moments later, when the shots arrived at their destination, the women, including Charlotte, smiled and waved as they tipped their petite glasses up to the sky.

"Now you go over there," Paul instructed Ryan.

"You guys gotta come with me," Ryan said.

"You can't do anything on your own, can you?" Paul said.

"This might be why you're single," Wes added, laughing.

The men grabbed their beers and walked over to the opposite side of the bar. A few other people were there, but it was nowhere near crowded.

"Thank you, Ryan," Piper smiled, getting up to hug him.

"Figured you wouldn't mind," Ryan said, returning the hug.

"Why are you guys out tonight?" Piper asked.

"Just hanging out," he said.

"Well, join us then!" Piper offered.

The girls smiled, and the guys pulled up some chairs. Wes turned to grab his beer, and when he turned back around, the only open spot was next to Charlotte.

"Hope you don't mind," Wes said, sitting down next to her.

"Not at all," Charlotte sweetly replied, their shoulders

touching.

The group started chatting, and the night slowly moved on. Drinks were shared, and laughs were flowing freely throughout the group as live music from the Wharf floated in through the open windows. Wes enjoyed carefree nights like this. He wondered if they were going to stop once he married Emily. She wasn't a fan of going out, much less a fan of Paul and Ryan. He only saw them when he wasn't working and Emily was back at her family's home in Martha's Vineyard, where she worked, a short ferry ride away from Newport. On a few occasions, she had urged him to move to Martha's Vineyard, but Wes could never imagine leaving this magical place. Emily didn't mind isolating him, and maybe that was what was causing his anxiety. She was slowly attempting to suffocate his freedom, something he was just beginning to realize.

As they sat at the table, the clinking of glasses and the murmur of conversation faded into the background, replaced by the rhythm of her voice—so steady, yet full of warmth. She spoke of her day at work and a funny little story about a forgotten wallet, and for a moment, everything else seemed to blur. His gaze, once casually drifting between friends, now anchored itself on her, as if drawn by some quiet gravity.

Her words, at first just moments of casual conversation, now seemed to carry weight. He found himself listening more intently, savoring the way she chose her words, how her thoughts flowed so seamlessly, her wit sharp yet soft. Every now and then, her gaze would meet his across the table, and for a split second, it felt like a quiet acknowledgment between two people who might have once been strangers but now shared something unspoken. There was a warmth about her as she interacted with everyone, something he had not yet seen but left him feeling undone.

"I think I'm gonna turn in," Charlotte announced, yawning.

"What?" Piper put a hand over hers. "Stay!"

"I'm exhausted," she insisted. "But I'll see you tomorrow at work."

"Fine," Piper moaned, rolling her eyes.

Wes watched Charlotte as she pulled her light jean jacket over her shoulders. Without thinking, he found himself standing up from his seat, the words slipping from his mouth before he could stop them: "Would you mind some company?"

She glanced at him, surprised, but not unwelcoming.

"Sure," Charlotte said.

Normally, Wes felt confident in keeping his distance from her, but tonight, something had shifted. Her laugh and the way she carried herself made his offer less of an obligation as a gentleman, but more like something he *wanted* to do.

Everyone was too buzzed to care as the two walked out to leave.

"I don't think we'll be missed," Charlotte said, descending the silver stairs that led them down to the main patio.

"I don't think so either," Wes laughed, following close behind her.

"Tonight was fun, though. I needed this," she said. "I didn't want to go, but Piper dragged me out."

"Me too," Wes sighed. "Work's so busy lately, I feel

like I never get out."

They noticed the Wharf winding down as well; other restaurants were starting to pack up their outdoor patios, a gentle end to a busy evening. The twinkle lights adorning the patios were still lit, the dark sky illuminating them. Charlotte looked up, smiling.

"You like it here?" Wes asked, noticing her happiness.

"I do," the curve of her lips seemed to grow larger on her petite face.

"It's a special place," he said, looking ahead.

They walked in silence for a bit. "Have you ever thought about leaving?" Charlotte asked..

"I did leave for medical school," he explained.

"Where did you go?" she asked.

"Baylor," he stated. "In Texas."

"How'd you like it there?"

"It was great, a small town just like here, except for a bunch of new people. I really contemplated staying there after graduation, but I found my way back here," he said.

They walked onto Mill Street, away from Bowen's Wharf.

"It was scary at first," he said. "But once I got settled, it felt like an extension of home."

"Moving away seems to highlight parts of yourself you didn't know you had," Charlotte added.

"Right," Wes said, "It was scary leaving the comforts of home."

"Exactly," Charlotte said.

"Was it scary leaving Seattle?" Wes asked.

"It was," she started. "But it wasn't until recently that

I unpacked a new sense of myself here, something I would have never been able to find in Seattle."

A car slowly passed, street lights embellishing the road beside them.

Wes slowed to match her pace.

Charlotte took an unexpected turn towards the harbor. She rested her arms on the railing just above the black water beneath them.

"I just can't get enough of it," she said, glancing forward at the water, its darkness entrancing her.

Wes took his place beside her, their bodies close to each other. He could sense her comfort; her body language relaxed.

"It's something I took for granted," he confessed.

"Sometimes we do that if we've been in a place too long," Charlotte said. "It's only natural."

Wes let their conversation stall, her words stringing between his ears. He couldn't help but relate that sentiment to Emily. They were so comfortable with each other, and they knew everything they could about the other. Emily had her flaws, but she had also been by his side for as long as he could remember. Before they were romantically involved, she had been his biggest supporter, his best friend. They often snuck out of their houses in the middle of the night as teens to see one another. They ran with the fireflies in the summertime, with no care in the world. Afterward, they would lay in the freshly mowed grass and stare at the twinkling stars. They wondered where their lives would take them and attempted to navigate the most perfect scenarios where they were still together. She had been his safety net when life got difficult, and he was her sounding board when she needed to vent. His biggest fear would be to take her and their memories for granted, after all that time. He felt like he owed her something, but was the rest of his life the answer?

It could have been the cocktails or the late hour, but he felt a pull towards Charlotte. The way she carried herself led him to believe she was self-aware and adventurous, which intrigued him. He desperately wanted to know more about her, but did not want to pry. Their two existences simultaneously found a home with one another on an unexpected Saturday night.

Charlotte leaned against him without thinking, her body drawn to his warmth. She began to feel the steady beat of his heart as she closed her eyes, letting herself rest for a moment. She was overwhelmed by the security his presence exuded.

But then, like a jolt of electricity, the reality hit her. *He's engaged.*

Her breath caught as the guilt spiraled through her, "I better get going. I have work in the morning, and I don't want Susan to wait up."

Wes was still, watching her with a quiet confusion. He noticed the space between them widening.

"She'll be fine," he said. "I bet you money that she's snoring on the couch when you walk in."

Charlotte chuckled at the thought, fizzling the tension between them, "I had a great night."

"Me too," Wes said. "Get home safe."

Wes watched as she walked away, the lamp above them forming her shadow on the street. She did not need a clear protector, but at that moment, he wondered how it would feel to walk beside her. He let himself linger in the thought, imagining what it would be like to close the distance between them, to step away from the boundaries of friendship and his impending marriage and into something uncharted, something that might either change everything or leave them both wondering what could have been.

Instead, he sighed, fumbling with his keys in his hands, as he walked back alone to his apartment nearby.

***

"I will never stop chasing you," Asher *whispered into her ear as they strolled along the smooth South Carolina beach, hand in hand.*

Charlotte paused and raised her chin to allow her eyes to meet his. She couldn't imagine a more perfect moment; his tenderness poured out of his heart to meet hers.

"And I'll protect you," he added.

"What if I don't need protection?" she asked.

"Oh, you will," he winked.

Just as quick as the romantic moment came, the winds pulled it away with the tide just as fast. His response hung above them as the pale moon did; his eagerness to shape her life was palpable. Before she could respond, his arms were wrapped around her waist, pulling her in for a kiss, as if to stop any reaction she wanted to have. Their hearts rose and fell with each passing moment as the sea rolled in, wetting their feet. Their faces came apart like a magnet, smiling and looking down at each other's saturated toes.

"Well," Asher said.

"Thankfully, we were carrying our shoes," Charlotte giggled.

"Shall we move up and have a seat?" Asher asked.

"Let's," Charlotte said.

As they walked up the sand to a higher location, safe from the water, they plopped down next to each other, marveling at the open sea.

"This is beautiful," Charlotte said.

Seagulls flew sporadically above them, cawing for any trace of food to devour.

"We used to come here every summer," Asher said. "My mom hated it when my brother and I fed the seagulls our boardwalk fries."

Charlotte laughed.

"It would start with just a few, but then, a whole bunch of them would show up."

"I bet it was fun, though," Charlotte said.

The breeze sailed between them, as a lock of Charlotte's hair that wasn't tied up in her bun, wisped and tickled her ear.

"What if we brought our kids here one day?" Asher said.

Charlotte stopped at the sentiment, and a smile appeared on her cheeks.

"Well, I'm sure they would feed the seagulls, too," she said.

"I would hope," he said. "I could see you now, sitting in your beach chair with your large sun hat waving them away."

"Oh, would I?" she asked. "And where would you be?"

"Helping them feed the seagulls, of course!"

They laughed as Charlotte noticed Asher's left leg extend out, his hand reaching into his pocket. Her heart stilled.

"I want you forever, Charlotte," he said. "And I can't see anyone else by my side."

Charlotte gasped and brought a hand to cover her mouth as a beautiful diamond ring appeared in front of her.

"Will you marry me?" Asher asked.

"Yes!" Charlotte said without hesitation.

Asher slipped the ring onto her finger as they kissed. His passion fueled hers, and she wished she could preserve the moment forever.

***

Newport, Rhode Island, Present Day: Charlotte

Charlotte giggled as she turned the key and saw Susan in her worn armchair. The flicker of the television cast soft shadows on the wall. Her slippered feet rested underneath her crocheted blanket, soft puffs of air escaping her mouth with each breath. Every now and then, she snorted, a wrinkle in her tranquility. Wes had been right.

She felt a sense of happiness wash over her as she walked toward her bedroom. She plopped down on her bed, back first. Her eyes shut, and her smile widened. Tonight had been unforeseen yet enjoyable. She had learned lately that it was what happened *without* a plan that made her most joyful. Something she would not have expected of herself in the past. She was a planner, someone who always knew her next step. This stage of life had led her to prove that she did not always need a plan. Learning as she lived proved to be more fun. As she shut her eyes, she couldn't help but feel so grateful for the life she was now leading.

The next morning, the birds outside her bedroom window awoke her like the most serene alarm clock. She rubbed her eyes with her hands as she steadily sat up. Still, in her clothes from the night before, she figured she'd get changed, go for a run, and enjoy a long shower.

As she stepped outside, the birds that had awakened her fluttered throughout the garden just outside the front door. The warm sun kissed her arm, welcoming her outside. She placed her AirPods in and turned her workout playlist up. She stretched a bit and started on her run. She had mentally mapped out her path as she laced her sneakers. She would go towards the cliff walk and run alongside the ocean for a bit. It turned out to be the perfect Sunday. A lot of other people had the same idea she had, taking advantage of the warm weather. As she crossed the historic district, she couldn't help but notice the historical mansions she was running by. Their distinct architecture marveled her. Some of them were quaint and sophisticated, while others were immense and gothic. Either way, she loved how well cared for most of them were.

The ocean appeared after a few blocks, and its beauty stopped her in her tracks. She stood to catch her breath, amazed at how blue the ocean could be. She thought she had appreciated it before, but its rocky disposition led to a beautiful abyss of navy brilliance. She stood off to the side and stretched a little more before continuing her run. The music she was listening to made her forget her lower back pain from not running as often as she used to back in Seattle. It was something that relieved her stress and anxious thoughts. The wind had picked up, the salty air running through her ponytail. Her hat was safely fastened onto her head, only moving a little bit. Other people were walking the trail, but it wasn't crowded.

After a few miles, she stopped to relieve some tension in her leg muscles. As she did, the image of Wes's smile from the night before flashed to the forefront of her mind. The memory of him washed over her like an endless tide, pulling her deeper into the current she knew she couldn't escape from.

Chapter 11

Seattle, Washington, Two Years Prior

"What the hell was that all about?" Asher yelled, slamming the front door, home at last.

Charlotte was silent, placing her clutch on the counter and reaching up for a water glass.

"I mean, that was uncalled for and embarrassing. Aren't you embarrassed?" he berated her.

"Not as embarrassed as *you* should be," she exclaimed, her words hung in the air, sharp and accusing.

Asher slammed his fist on the counter, flushed with anger.

"I wouldn't have said any of that if you had been honest with me in the first place. Did I take it too far? Maybe. But guess what? I wanted answers," she explained.

"You have no right, no right to be all up in my business," Asher reminded her.

"We're married, Asher. I'm allowed to be all up in your business," she repeated, her voice trembling with a mix of defiance and hurt.

They were silent as Charlotte plucked his laptop off the counter, making her way to the couch.

"What are you doing?" he asked.

"Finding out once and for all," she answered. She sat

down and moved the mouse, springing the screen to life, typing in his password.

His intense anger was palpable; she could feel his demise crashing towards her like waves in a storm.

After logging in, she clicked on the email symbol. Her heart felt like it was going to explode as the blood in her veins pumped her body with adrenaline. She knew she was right, but she needed *him* to know he couldn't hide anything from her. She scrolled through and found the email chain between him and Rebecca under the label "Important." She scoffed out loud, realizing his game. He thought hiding it under that label would deter her from the contents of their thread, concealing it as "business" related. Her eyes darted back and forth, their conversations sending daggers toward her heart.

You were always mine.

Her body heaved as his truth was revealed, his words slicing through her heart like a knife.

She has no idea.

Charlotte's angry eyes flashed to Asher.

"You humiliated me," he growled. "You've ruined everything."

Her stomach twisted at the venom in his words. For a brief, horrifying moment, she wondered if he had truly believed he had done nothing wrong. The tension between them crackled, thick and suffocating as she realized his anger wasn't directed at the betrayal; it was now turned on her.

"I can't do this," she said. "Kate always told me you couldn't be trusted. I always knew you were never completely happy with me."

"Charlotte," he said, his tone shifting.

She grabbed her water glass and threw it onto the floor, the glass shattering into a million pieces.

"I hate you," she scowled.

***

"I'm taking you out tonight," Kate said into the phone. "Meet me at Buxston's downtown, 5:30 pm."

"Okay," Charlotte said into the phone, "see you then."

Charlotte closed down her computer and walked out of her tiny office. She grabbed her bag and said goodbye to the general manager of the restaurant, "See you Monday!" she smiled.

As she walked onto the ferry that would take her back to the city from Bainbridge Island, she closed her eyes and breathed in the salty air. The seagulls above her cawed as the sea lions barked on the banks of the island. The green water lapped up against the ship as it started to move, her senses in overdrive. Asher had said he would be in a late meeting and would hopefully be joining her afterward for the ferry ride home. She hoped he wouldn't be delayed, as he often was.

Once in the city, she stepped off the ferry and briskly walked down the street to Buxston's. Thankfully, it was only a few blocks away, so it wasn't too much of an inconvenience for her. As Charlotte got close to the entrance of the bar, Kate stepped out of a cab and onto the sidewalk.

"Perfect timing," she smiled at her friend.

"Oh, I've had a day!" Kate gushed, engulfing her friend in a hug. "Let's get a drink."

The two women walked arm in arm. It looked a little crowded, but they quickly found a high-top table only a few feet from the bar.

"Would you ladies like anything to drink?" the waitress asked, walking over and dropping drink menus on the table in front *of them.*

"Of course," Kate sighed with a smile, losing the scarf around her neck, "we would both like a glass of your house white."

"Perfect," she said. "I'll be back with that shortly."

"I needed this," Charlotte smiled, looking around the bar.

"I know you did," Kate said. "How was Kiawah? You barely replied to any of my texts."

Charlotte hadn't told anybody she and Asher were engaged, but decided she couldn't hide it any longer. She slid her sleeve up, extending her hand across the table to her friend, her engagement ring the star of the show.

"What!" Kate exclaimed.

"He proposed," Charlotte said.

Kate spit her wine back into her glass, letting out a cough of disbelief.

"Oh my god," Kate said, placing Charlotte's hand in hers so she could get a better look at it.

"I know, it's actually kind of heavy," Charlotte said.

"It's beautiful," she said.

"His proposal was so sweet and kind of unexpected," Charlotte said as Kate coughed again, looking past her.

"What is wrong with you?" Charlotte asked, starting to laugh.

"What time did Asher say his meeting was ending?" Kate asked, dropping Charlotte's hand.

Charlotte glanced at her phone.

"He's still in his meeting," she answered.

"Are you sure about that?" Kate said, nodding her head to the corner of the bar.

Charlotte turned around, and her heart fell to the floor. Her mouth gaped open as she quickly turned back to her friend, her heart racing.

"Who is he with?" Kate asked, her eyes darting from Charlotte to Asher.

"I don't know," Charlotte cowered, as she slowly turned her head for a better look.

Charlotte could not believe her eyes. She recognized a few of his male colleagues, but the woman he was with was unfamiliar to her. Her curly blonde hair and little black dress revealed her tiny, slender figure. The two were standing dangerously close to one another, his back against the bar as she sat in the swivel chair beside him. As she laughed, her back brushed up against Asher's chest, something he was enjoying.

"Is he for real right now?" Kate asked, her anger growing.

Charlotte noticed Asher was too close for comfort. She saw him lower his head, whispering something to this woman. She noticed his smile as he pulled away; this woman's laugh echoed throughout the room.

"I'm going over there," Kate said, taking a long sip of her wine and emptying it.

"No, no," Charlotte pleaded as Kate stepped down from her chair.

Charlotte buried her face in her hands.

"Hey Asher," Kate said with confidence.

Charlotte groaned, shutting her eyes and instantly wishing she were somewhere else.

"Kate!" he smiled, unfazed.

"Yeah, I'm here with your fiancée, remember her?" Kate huffed.

"Charlotte? Where?" She could hear the fake joy flowing

through his words.

"We're sitting over there. Maybe once you're done flirting, you could join us," she said.

"Kate, I'm not – " he said as Kate walked back to Charlotte.

"He is something else, I swear," she said, fuming.

Charlotte looked up at her friend, her eyes welling up with tears.

She was mortified.

***

Newport, Rhode Island, Present Day: Wes

"I think I'm going to stay here in Martha's Vineyard," Emily voiced over the phone. "I have so much work to do and can't seem to get away right now."

Wes had just awoken, enjoying his hot cup of coffee on his balcony that overlooked the harbor. With the phone pressed against his ear, his fingers tapped absentmindedly on the edge of the ledge, his gaze unfocused. The conversation drifted on the other end. Changing to issues with the wedding vendors and a scheduling issue with the band they had selected, a steady stream of words that seemed to go on without much meaning. Every now and then, he murmured a polite "Mm-hmm" or "Right," but his tone was flat, detached, nothing more than a soft acknowledgment to fill the silence.

He glanced down at his watch. He needed to get going as he didn't want to be late for work.

"Alright, well, I love you, I'll keep you in the loop on when I can get away and visit you."

"Sounds good, love you too," she said.

Click.

***

Seattle, Washington, Two Years Prior

Charlotte bypassed the broken glass and slammed his laptop back on the island.

"There, you can have it back," she growled.

A text appeared on his phone.

How is she? – Rebecca asked.

Asher knew Rebecca was the last person he should be talking to, but she gave him comfort, and he gave in to the temptation.

Emotional – he answered.

Asher quickly followed behind Charlotte as she trudged up the stairs.

"We need to talk about this," he pleaded.

"You're the last person I want to talk to," she said.

As they changed into their pajamas, in complete silence, Charlotte sighed as she got into bed. Her body ached, and her chest was sore from crying. Both pillars in her life were crashing to the ground, leaving Charlotte with the feeling of paralyzing instability.

The darkness in the room was unbearable; the storm in her heart was beginning to emerge once again. Asher turned on the floor lamp in the corner of their room, Charlotte's eyes squinted.

"Please leave," she pleaded with him.

"Let's work this out," he said, sitting up, his cell phone continuously pinging.

"Is that Rebecca?" Charlotte questioned.

There was a long pause.

Charlotte sighed, shutting her eyes, questioning everything.

With a voice raw and seething, she pointed to the door, her words cutting through the air like a knife, "Get out of my room — now."

The next day, Charlotte's eyes were red-rimmed and tired as she stared blankly at her mug full of coffee. She noticed a few tears that were suspended in her lashes. She glanced over to the couch where Asher was mindlessly scrolling through his phone, distant and self-absorbed. His shoulders were relaxed, unaware, as though the world had not shifted beneath him. She caught herself looking at him, her chest tightening with a mix of longing and frustration. She wanted to speak, to tell him that she felt lost, that the ache inside her was deeper than words, but the space between them felt insurmountable.

She shifted slightly, the weight of her loss heavy in her bones, and for a moment, she wondered if he even noticed the emptiness in her eyes. He heard the spoon clink against her mug and glanced over at her. However, it wasn't with the softness she longed for, but a fleeting glance before he returned to his phone.

The silence between them stretched again, only distancing them further away from each other.

***

Newport, Rhode Island, Present Day: Charlotte

Charlotte emerged from the shower after her run, the heat from the water permeating her skin. She had work soon and was looking forward to it. After drying her hair and pulling on her sundress, she applied light makeup and headed for the door. She told herself she would grab a cup of coffee before her shift started.

Mainsail was pretty busy, buzzing with life, but the warmth it exuded wrapped around her like a cashmere blanket. The rich aroma of freshly ground beans and steamed milk filled the air, mingling with the faint scent of pastries and cinnamon. The hum of quiet chatter blended well with the clinking of mugs and the hiss of the espresso machine. As she stood in line, contemplating her order, she couldn't help but notice the buttery sunlight streaming in from the window.

"Debbie left us with a few tasks, so if we knock those out, we should be easy sailing the rest of the day," Piper said behind her.

"Okay," Charlotte said.

The two paid and grabbed their coffees, making their way to Finnegan's. Piper was, as always, full of energy and sharing a funny story about the night before, when she opened the door to the store and fell silent.

They stepped inside, the soft click of their shoes on the hardwood floor echoing in the empty shop. The bright displays of neatly arranged children's clothes, once carefully curated, now looked disordered, as if an invisible hand had swept through and torn them apart. Shirts and pants were scattered across the floor, some crumpled in twisted piles, others hanging loosely from half-empty racks.

The mirrors, polished and pristine just the day before, were smudged, as if someone had been sifting through the piles of clothes. The register area, usually so organized, looked as though it had been rummaged through in a hurry; papers were scattered, receipts and price tags were torn, and the once organized counter was now left in disarray.

A few hangers had been knocked from their hooks, dangling awkwardly as though left in a hurry. The back room door was ajar, a small sliver of shadow spilling into the main shop, as if something had been disturbed there, too.

They stood still for a moment, taking in the sight, the weight of the loss pressing down on them.

"We have to call Debbie," Piper whispered, unsettled.

Chapter 12

Newport, Rhode Island, Present Day: Charlotte

Susan opened the door to let Charlotte through the entryway, as she was finishing up watering her potted plants on the doorstep.

"I've been craving your iced tea," Charlotte sighed. "It was a long day."

"Well, you're lucky I still have some in the fridge. Wes loves it too."

Charlotte pretended not to notice his name lingering, like a quiet vibration, in her mind. Something in her chest tightened, a small flicker of recognition. It wasn't a feeling that demanded attention, but it also wasn't easy to ignore.

As the two made their way into the kitchen, Susan poured the beloved iced tea into a glass, and they both stepped onto the back balcony.

"What happened? Why was it a long day?" Susan asked.

"The store got broken into," Charlotte said. "It's terrible."

Susan's eyes widened. "That's awful. How is Debbie faring?"

"Not good, as to be expected. Piper and I stayed late trying to put everything back together and checking inventory, but the safe in the back room was broken into. I swear I saw Debbie's eyes tearing up as soon as she got to the store," Charlotte explained. "I'm not supposed to be working tomorrow, but I'm going in anyway to help."

"There has to be something we can do," Susan said. "Maybe we can raise money somehow for her. You know what?" her eyes widened. " Every year, I have a Fourth of July barbecue. Maybe we can make it into a charity event?"

"That's a wonderful idea," Charlotte remarked. "I can help you if you want. I used to work in marketing, planning a party is kind of my thing."

"You wouldn't mind?" Susan asked.

"Not at all, it would be fun."

As the two chatted, Charlotte couldn't help but feel grateful. Grateful for the positive people in her life and optimistic for whatever lay ahead. She loved the idea of planning a party, something she missed at her old job. She enjoyed booking vendors and thinking of ways to pull everything together, sometimes in a pinch. In college, she was an assistant to a well-known wedding planner in her hometown. She taught Charlotte all about time management, budgets, and how to keep lasting relationships with others. Having good relationships with caterers and venues was imperative in both wedding planning and the PR work she did at the restaurant. It was all about the connections you shared with others that made the difference in making your clients' visions come to life.

"First, we need to make a list of things we need, and then we can work on a guest list," Charlotte instructed.

"There are so many artists around here, maybe we can

get a few to donate their pieces for a silent auction," Susan explained.

"I love that!" Charlotte responded.

Susan got up and went inside. She came back with some paper and a pen.

"Let's start with the guest list," she beamed.

***

Newport, Rhode Island, Present Day: Wes

As Wes awoke, he stretched his arm towards his phone to shut off his alarm. The morning light filtered softly through the curtains. He threw off the covers, sitting up, as a yawn escaped his mouth. He swung his feet to the cold hardwood floor, squinting his eyes at the morning light. A quick shower and a small cup of espresso were all he needed as motivation to start his workday.

After pulling on his hospital scrubs, he walked into the kitchen to turn on his espresso machine when his phone lit up.

It was Emily.

"Good morning," he said, placing the phone to his ear.

"Morning," she stated.

"How is everything?" he asked, placing his espresso pod into the machine.

"Good, I'm very focused. I'm getting a lot of work done," she explained.

"Good," he said, watching the hot espresso drip slowly into his mug.

"So I was talking to my mom yesterday…" she started to explain as Wes's mind wandered.

As she talked about wedding plans and details, Wes could feel his chest tightening. It was always a frantic swirl of decisions, timelines, and expectations that never seemed to stop. It was a slow build-up to a mounting pressure that seemed to seep into every corner of his life. He wanted to be involved, but the close relationship between Emily and her mother prevented it. He wished Emily would come to him first, not come to him second. Every conversation with family or friends about the wedding felt like another reminder of how many things had to be *perfect*. There was no room for imperfection, no space for mistakes. Every tiny detail seemed so critical, each choice so final.

"So what do you think?" she asked. "Buffet or sit down? My mom wants a more formal sit-down dinner with waiters."

Silence filled the air between them.

"Wes?"

"Honestly, I think buffet."

"I knew you were going to say that," she spat.

"I know it's a formal event, but I just see a buffet being easier," Wes explained.

Emily grew silent.

"I'll take your opinion into consideration," she said.

"Thank you," he said.

"Well, I have another phone call coming in. I'll talk to you later."

"Sounds good," he said.

He tapped the screen to end the conversation. He took a sip of his espresso and walked out onto his small patio. The light breeze caressed his arms as he watched a bird dive towards the whitecaps in the distance, as waves lapped up against the dock two floors beneath him.

A knot started to form in his chest, one that he could not untangle. He constantly felt he was on edge, as if standing on a cliff, looking down at something monumental, and realizing you weren't sure you were ready to jump. The wedding was supposed to be a celebration, but now it felt more like a performance, and they were the stars of the show.

He had a few minutes before he had to head into the hospital, so he grabbed his notebook and pen from inside and returned to the patio. Whenever he felt like this, channeling it into music always calmed the storm.

***

Newport, Rhode Island, Present Day: Charlotte & Wes

The moment she stepped through the door to Finnegan's, it creaked softly, announcing her arrival. It was all hands on deck as she saw Piper and Debbie placing usable inventory into boxes, preparing them for reorganization. A few other people were there to help, Debbie's husband included.

"We'll find out who did this," Debbie's husband reminded her.

"I hope so," she murmured, placing her hands on her hips, observing the destruction.

Charlotte placed her purse behind the counter. "Where do you want me?" Charlotte asked.

"Honestly, anywhere. Can you start over in the back of the store? We're just trying to organize things into sizes right now," Debbie explained.

"I can do that," she said.

As the clock ticked way past closing time, the only other sound Charlotte could hear was the soft hum of the streetlights outside as darkness enveloped Newport. The chaos from the destruction had cleared away, its remnants still lingered in the air, but the items had found new homes on the shelves. The clutter had been cleared as Charlotte sat alone at the counter, sifting through inventory lists, her face illuminated by the soft light of the desk lamp. Her hair was drawn up in a claw clip, messy after a long day of cleaning. She rolled up her sleeves as she picked up Debbie's receipt book to verify recent purchases. Debbie and Piper had been exhausted, so Charlotte offered to stay behind and close up shop.

It wasn't until she heard the click of boots against the floor that she looked up, her dark rimmed glasses falling low on her nose.

"Hey," Wes said softly, stepping inside. "It's late, you're still here?"

Charlotte rubbed her temples with a sigh, "There's still so much to go through, I don't want to leave this all for Debbie to figure out. She has so much on her plate."

Wes smiled, his easy, disarming grin that seemed to make things less heavy. "Well, you're in luck," he said.

"What?" she asked.

"Coffee," he said, pulling out a second cup, setting it on the counter next to Charlotte. "The good kind, trust me, this is exactly what you need right now."

She glanced at the coffee, hesitating for a beat, with tired eyes. Her fingers brushed his as she raised the cup to her lips. The rich scent of dark roast beans eased the tension in her head. "Thank you."

"I saw you in here on my way home from the hospital. I figured you needed a break."

Wes shrugged, casually leaning against the counter in an effortless way that always made him seem in control, yet approachable. He reached for a few scattered papers on the counter. "You're not doing this alone, not while I'm here."

Charlotte glanced at him, surprised by his calm demeanor and his ability to take charge without making her feel helpless.

"Fine," she said. "Only because I can't see straight right now. I've been running numbers for too long."

Wes smiled, "Deal. I'll help you tackle this paperwork, and you mop whatever dust is left on the floor. We'll get everything cleaned up so you can finally go home and rest."

Charlotte took another sip of her coffee and could feel the stress slide off her shoulders. She watched as he moved strategically, as if he had worked here for years, diving in as though it were natural to him. She shook her head, almost in disbelief.

"How do you do it?" she asked.

Wes met her gaze, a playful glint in his eye. "Do what?"

"Take charge. You just walked in here and you've got everything figured out."

He tilted his head while straightening his back. "For what it's worth," he said, his expression softening, "sometimes the people who look like they have it all together are just as lost, we're just better at pretending."

"Well," she said. "Thank you for pretending for me

tonight."

"Anytime," he whispered, his eyes catching hers.

As they worked together in the quiet of the night, something shifted between them. Even though the numbers still didn't add up and there was still plenty of missing inventory, somehow with Wes there, everything seemed a little less daunting.

With their unspoken feelings hanging between them, they both couldn't help but wonder where this connection could lead.

"I have an idea," Wes said. "I want to show you somewhere you haven't been yet. Meet me at Mainsail in the morning."

Charlotte's tired eyes followed him with admiration, as if he knew the answer to everything. "Sure," she said.

***

Newport, Rhode Island, Present Day: Charlotte & Wes

The morning air was crisp, brushing its cool tendrils across her cheeks. Standing at the edge of the dock, Charlotte leaned forward, resting her forearms on the weathered wood of the railing. She curled her hands around her cappuccino, the steam rising in delicate swirls into the salty breeze. She glanced down at her watch, anticipating Wes's arrival.

As she stood there, alone, she noticed how peaceful the stillness of the early summer morning was. A few boats bobbed in the harbor, their sails furling in the quiet morning breeze. The sweet fragrance of blossoming flowers grounded her as her gaze became lost in the rhythm of the lapping water against the dock. She took a slow sip of her coffee, its warmth filling her from the inside. Her eyes flickered toward the horizon, its golden hues reaching across the water, as if to welcome her in. It was a moment of quiet connection, as if she were anchored to this place.

"Charley!"

She turned to see a smiling Wes approaching her.

"Sorry, I'm late," he said. "The sunrise was too good to miss."

"I should have known," she said, shaking her head as a smile tugged at the edges of her lips.

"You ready for your surprise?" he grinned mischievously.

"Is it a boat ride?" she asked, raising her eyebrows.

"You can keep guessing all you want," he shrugged. "But you're going to have to wait and see."

He led her over to his car parked on the edge of the street.

"Is it far?" she asked. Her eyes playfully narrowed as they walked down the street, trying to read the grin on his face.

Wes only smiled, tapping the roof of his car as they approached it.

"Just trust me," he said.

Moments later, Wes's car rolled smoothly along Ocean Drive, the salty air brushing against their windows. Charlotte leaned back against the seat, her eyes wide as the view of the ocean unfolded before them. The sparkling blue water shimmered like diamonds as sailboats paraded gracefully across the horizon, their white sails catching the breeze and slicing through the water like delicate strokes of a brush on canvas.

"I've never seen anything like this," Charlotte whispered.

"I promise, it gets better," he said, turning the car onto a narrow driveway.

"Where are we going?" she asked.

"Ever heard of Castle Hill Lighthouse?" he asked.

Charlotte shook her head as Wes pulled into the small parking lot next to the Castle Hill Inn. The car's engine fell silent as they parked, now perched on the scenic peninsula overlooking Narragansett Bay. The Inn was beautiful, its stunning blend of historic charm and coastal elegance reflected the nearby sea.

"I figured after I show you the lighthouse, we can get a bite to eat here at the Inn. I know a guy," he smirked.

"I'm sure you do," Charlotte giggled, her eyes still stuck on the beauty of the grounds before them.

The large stone terrace seemed inviting as her eyes followed the sea of white adirondack chairs ornamenting the large lawn overlooking the bay.

"Okay, seriously, what are you showing me?" she asked.

"It's a little spot I like to go to, where the world gets quiet." He looked at her then, in a way that made her heart skip a little.

Charlotte raised her eyebrows and nodded as they exited his car. She followed him down a narrow dirt path, greenery encapsulating them in time. Wild flowers popped through a thick canopy of thin branches that hung above them as they padded atop the soft undergrowth. Charlotte turned her head, and a sudden movement caught her eye, a flutter of wings.

Dancing among the branches, a group of tiny birds chirped in whimsical grace. Their soft and light feathers quivered in the cool shadows of the trees, stopping Charlotte in her tracks. A calm settled over her as she watched them, reminding her of the simple magic in these quiet moments of life.

"You okay?" Wes asked, glancing behind his shoulder.

"Yeah," she said, continuing on.

As they rounded the curve of the path, the lighthouse came into view. Its white granite tower stood in stark contrast to the navy blue ocean behind it. It was resting on the rocky side of the hill overlooking the bay, a slim staircase snaking towards the private beach below it.

Charlotte stepped forward, at the crest of the hill, her breath catching as she looked out over the ocean that seemed to blend seamlessly with the sky. Her world, for once, felt distant and soft. The hustle of daily life faded into the background as the quiet breeze felt almost tangible, wrapping around her and calming her senses. A swell of emotion, as soft as the waves beneath them, washed over her. Tears welled in her eyes, not from sorrow, but from an overwhelming joy she had never felt before. It was as if the world had revealed something she had unknowingly been searching for. A quiet sob escaped her lips as she smiled through the tears, letting them fall softly down her cheeks. In that moment, she felt small, yet utterly connected to herself and to the world surrounding her.

Wes stood behind her, steady and aware, as he watched her cry. He didn't move, he didn't rush to console her, he didn't want to take this moment away from her. He sensed the deep feelings of her past, the ones she's hidden for so long, flow from her eyes. It was a silent confession that seemed both painful and beautiful, like a dam finally breaking. He stepped closer, his heart heavy with an emotion he didn't quite have the words to express. He understood that this moment, fragile and fleeting, was something neither of them had expected. In this release, he saw a beauty so intimate, it almost took his breath away.

***

Newport, Rhode Island, Present Day: Wes

"Do you need any help setting up?" Susan asked Wes, her margarita safely in her left hand.

Wes smiled, "No, Grandma, you just take your seat and enjoy yourself."

"Oh, I will," she laughed, taking a swig of her sweet drink.

"Hey, Susan!" Charlotte smiled, walking up to them.

"Charlotte," Susan beamed, noticing Wes' eyes brightening. "How are you?"

"Good! I drafted up the invitation for the Fourth of July party. They are turning out wonderful. I'll show them to you later," she explained.

"Invitations?" Wes asked, taking his guitar out of its case.

"Yes, for our Fourth of July party," Charlotte said.

"Bringing those back?" Wes asked.

"I want to," Susan said. "It was one of your grandfather's favorite traditions, and we really need to help Debbie out.

Finnegan's has been around a while."

"I think that's a great idea. Do you want me and the guys to perform?" Wes asked.

"Oh, would you?" her words spilling out quickly, unable to contain her excitement.

"Yes," he said. "How many people are you inviting to this thing?"

"Whoever wants to come," Susan said. "It'll be fun!"

People started to file into the harbor, many getting drinks and grabbing their seats.

"Good luck," Charlotte whispered to Wes.

"Thanks," he said, taking his place on the small stage.

"Charlotte!" Piper yelled, causing her to turn away.

"Hi Piper!" Charlotte said.

As everyone took their seats, Wes started to sing. His two friends played alongside him. The twinkle lights beamed above them, illuminating the dark sky. Laughter filled the Wharf, and Wes's troubles faded away like the shore during low tide.

After a few songs, it was time for Wes to debut his new one. He went back and forth throughout the first half of his set. He wasn't convinced his new song was ready, and it didn't feel like the right time, but he told his band to fall back, leaving only Wes and his guitar on the small stage.

"This is a song I've recently written," he said into the mic, "hope you enjoy it."

His fingers lightly strummed the guitar, and the beginnings of the song filled the air. The soft and slow melody drifted sweetly among the harbor, and everybody quieted.

The days seem long without you near,
The days drag on, they do my dear.
You move like water upon my wave,
Your closeness I always seem to crave.

The notes he played were gentle as they floated into the air. They were delicate but with purpose. There was a certain rawness in the way his hands moved, his fingers strong and calloused from years of surgeries, but here, they were steady and controlled. Each strum was deliberate, never rushed. The quiet hum of the strings contrasted with the calm intensity in his posture. He wasn't trying to soften himself, but in this moment, the music was like a conversation meant for *someone* else.

You have no idea your effect on me,
Your soul is so bright, the sweetest I've seen.
I need you like a boat to the sea,
Your waves brushed fast against me.

As his eyes opened, coincidentally, they were met with Charlotte's. He could sense the tension coiling in the air between them. His throat tightened, and he could feel a warmth creeping up his neck, a flush that didn't belong. In that brief moment of their anxious dance of glances and evasions, they realized something they hadn't wanted to admit: *They couldn't stop looking at one another.* And for a moment, even trying to look away felt like a small betrayal of whatever it was that was beginning to take root deep inside them. He continued to sing, as if to only her. As he strummed the final notes and could hear the soft clapping of the audience, he looked down at his guitar.

I need a stiff drink, he thought.

***

Newport, Rhode Island, Present Day: Charlotte

His voice seemed to lull the conversations around the Wharf. Everyone quieted and listened to Wes. Charlotte couldn't take her eyes off him. His eyes were shut as he was fully immersed in the song. She recognized his passion; this was truly who he was. The twinkle lights above him highlighted the light perspiration on his forehead and chest, his buttoned shirt slightly opened. As he swayed with the music, his shirt moved slightly, revealing a nautical compass tattoo directly on his heart. She wondered if that compass charted the parts of his life that had already occurred or represented alternative paths for his future. Either way, the summer weather was warming everybody's bodies and spirits.

The days seem long without you near,
The days drag on, they do my dear.

Wes opened his eyes, and Charlotte met his. It was like an invisible thread, pulling her attention in his direction, despite every rational part of her mind telling her not to. She shifted slightly in her seat, hands folded tightly in her lap, trying to focus on anything else happening around her. The laughter, the clinking of glasses, it all felt distant, muffled, as if the air had thickened between them.

He was engaged, *engaged,* with someone else, and

that was a boundary she couldn't cross, especially after her experience with infidelity. Her breath hitched in her throat as she fought the overwhelming urge to look again. She felt the weight of what was unspoken, the silent ache that came with knowing what she couldn't have.

Susan nudged Charlotte, "He wrote this?" she asked.

"I guess so," Charlotte said.

"It's beautiful."

"Yes, it is," Charlotte smiled.

***

Newport, Rhode Island, Present Day: Charlotte

As Charlotte got up to leave, Wes quietly walked over to her and delicately touched her elbow.

"Did you have fun tonight?" he asked, his warm breath seemed to kiss her skin, laced with bourbon.

"I loved that song you wrote," she said, keeping some distance between them.

"Thank you," he said. "Kind of nerve-racking."

"Why?" she asked.

"It's a personal song, so I just hoped everyone enjoyed it."

"Well, everyone did, I can tell you that," she assured him.

"Would you like to go for a walk?" he asked.

She exhaled slowly, trying to calm the fluttering in her stomach. The words were there, waiting, but they felt like a heavy stone in her mouth. She didn't want to go for a walk with him, not because she didn't enjoy his company, not because she didn't like him, but because *she did*. And that was the problem. He was engaged. He had Emily. And her feelings for him, as much as they had been growing, as much as she wished she could ignore them, were still something she couldn't act on.

"Sure," she said quickly, grabbing her cardigan and pushing her chair in.

The words had spilled out before she could stop them, impulsivity now dictating her actions. The Wharf was shutting down after a fun-filled evening. Some people lingered, finishing their conversations and cocktails. The light breeze sent goosebumps up Charlotte's arm and a soft chill up her spine.

"Nights like these are my favorite," Wes said, holding onto his guitar case as they walked along the red brick walkway. They passed by Mainsail, a closed sign hanging on its door, slowly swaying with the breeze.

"I can see why," she said.

A brief pause lingered in the air between them.

"I think what you're planning with my grandmother is perfect. You have given her so much happiness, thank you," he said.

Her eyes held his for just a beat longer, as if the connection between them deepened in that shared sentiment.

"She's helped me so much, more than anyone knows."

He noticed it immediately, the way her smile faltered, how her eyes darted away from his. He could've pressed on, asked her more about her past, but something in the way she was withdrawing made him realize that this wasn't the time.

They both stood still at the base of Trinity Church Park, their necks arched up to the sky. Charlotte could sense the romanticity of the moment, but reminded herself he was taken. She did not want to jeopardize that, as awful a woman as Emily was. Wes looked down at her, taking a step towards her, closing the distance between them. Charlotte kept her gaze on the stars. A small crowd of people passed by, patting Wes on the back. He stepped back as they approached them.

"Good job tonight," one said.

"You still got it," another interjected.

"Thanks, guys," Wes humbly smiled, shifting his feet back towards Charlotte. "High school buddies," he explained.

"You have groupies," Charlotte said.

Wes laughed, "I think they all feel bad for me, that's really why they show up."

"That can't be true," Charlotte said. "Have you played live anywhere else?"

"I played a few times in college bars back at Baylor, but not as often as I do here," he said.

"You're more comfortable here," she said. "It shows."

Wes put his guitar down to sit on the stone wall bench just beside them. He hoped this would elongate their discussion. Charlotte did the same, crossing her legs. They could hear the screeching of cicadas humming in the distance as the moths gathered around the streetlights. A sliver of a smile set on both of their faces as the wind brushed salt on their skin. A wave of peace washed over their souls.

"It's funny how simple it all can be," Charlotte said.

Wes turned to look at her, and his attention piqued.

"Once you slow it all down," she explained. "Everything becomes more simple."

He smiled softly, the corners of his mouth turning up

with a quiet confidence.

"I'm sorry, I'm rambling," she said.

"Why are you apologizing?" he said. "It's how you feel."

She didn't say a word as she nodded in agreement. She thought about his words and how true they were. She was always so quick to apologize. Either it was for something she said or for simply taking up space.

"I'm working on that," she said.

Wes playfully nudged her shoulder as they looked out towards the water. The foggy haze that was emerging from the clouds in the distance signaled a rainy day ahead.

"Well, I'd better get going," Charlotte tapped her knees. "Have a good night, Wes."

"You too, Charley," he said.

She stood up and turned on her heels as she walked away, her arms crossed in front of her chest. She knew she could not love a man who belonged to another, for her heart recognized the quiet honor in his promise. With their connection growing, Charlotte knew she had to be careful. She did not wish to repeat Rebecca's mistakes. After all, they still haunted her.

Chapter 13

Seattle, Washington, Two Years Prior

After a few days of wallowing, Charlotte decided that she desperately needed to take a shower.

"Oh, good, you're up today," Asher said, walking into the bathroom as Charlotte got into the shower.

She sighed, ignoring him, giving in to the warm water crashing down her body.

Asher moved around the bathroom with hesitant steps. The silence between them was heavy and suffocating. He wasn't sure how to respond, so instead, he remained silent. They hadn't had a civil conversation since their dinner date, like two ships sailing past each other in the night.

The water gently fell down her skin, the suds cleansing her body. She couldn't deny how good the shower felt; her body renewed a bit. She hadn't looked up or acknowledged his presence, the betrayal sinking deeper into her bones. Her brain felt covered in fog; no matter how hard she tried, there were no words worthy enough to say.

"Are you...okay?" he asked.

Charlotte rolled her eyes and covered her face with her hands. The jealousy taking over her thoughts was too much to handle. He waited for a response, but nothing came. A flicker of frustration crossed his face, but disappeared quickly, replaced with the strained expression of guilt. It could have been the fear of her shutting him out completely, losing her more than he already has.

"I'm sorry, but I don't know what you want me to say," she said.

"I'm sorry, I know…"

She cut him off, her voice hollow. "Sorry doesn't change what you did."

His face hardened, but he didn't argue. Instead, he turned to leave.

Whatever strength she had mustered instantly crumbled within her. She sat down on the tile floor of the shower, sobbing. She let all of her frustration go, her mind whirling.

Asher was downstairs by this time, leaving her alone to cope with the unimaginable.

***

Newport, Rhode Island, Present Day: Charlotte & Wes

It was the day of Susan's Fourth of July party, and Charlotte could not contain her excitement. She was showered and comfortable in her blue and white gingham sundress, her hair effortlessly pulled back in a low bun. It was warmer than she expected it to be in Rhode Island, but she welcomed it.

It was nearing 3:00, and the party was set to start at 3:30. Charlotte grabbed a few last-minute party decorations she had bought. She placed them in a wooden crate and made her way to the backyard. When she arrived, Susan was frantic, pacing around the yard, checking the food and beverage station, and making sure the bartender knew the signature drink by heart.

"I've taste-tested it more than a few times," Susan admitted, acknowledging Charlotte's presence.

"What's wrong?" Charlotte asked, glancing around the yard. "Everything looks wonderful."

"It does? You sure?" she asked, a worried look staining her face."I don't want to let Debbie down, plus my late husband always had everything perfect, I don't want people to compare."

"They won't," Charlotte reassured her. "Besides, everyone is looking forward to it. The auctioneer just arrived. This will be fun."

Within a few minutes, guests were streaming in, dressed in their most festive red, white, and blue outfits. It wasn't long before the warm evening air hummed with the sound of soft laughter and clinking glasses as guests chatted about under the glow of string lights. At the heart of the celebration, a long, rustic wooden table was lined with vibrant canvases, each one a unique reflection of the community; bold brushstrokes of subtle watercolors of local landscapes. There were also a few nautical photos of sailboats that caught Charlotte's eye. It was the most perfect way to raise money for Finnegan's.

Wes's band was playing in the background while he enjoyed an evening with his grandmother, friends, and community.

"Grandma, this turned out awesome," he said, taking a long swig of his lemonade cocktail.

"You think? I think so too," she winked.

"Finally," Charlotte chimed in. "You're seeing how

fun this is now."

"I know, I know," Susan sighed. "I just wanted it all to come together."

"I don't think you have to worry about that," Wes smiled, watching everyone mingle and peruse the paintings that were being auctioned off.

Susan excused herself, and Charlotte refreshed her beverage and walked over to a table, taking a seat. She noticed Wes followed suit, pulling out a chair next to her.

Charlotte sipped on her refreshingly crisp white wine.

"Have you tried the boozy lemonade?" Wes asked.

"Not yet, but I heard it's potent," Charlotte laughed.

"Definitely is," Wes said, taking another sip.

"Susan worked hard on this party. I'm so glad she's finally having fun," Charlotte said, nodding towards Susan, who was joining her friends on the dance floor.

"This lemonade probably helped," Wes laughed. "But seriously, thank you so much for helping her. You did a great job, and not just with this party. She tells me how often she enjoys your company. She was all by herself before you and I worried about her often. My schedule is so erratic, but I always try to check up on her whenever I'm free."

"It's refreshing to meet people so kind," she said, curling her hair behind her ear. "In Seattle, I was surrounded by people who I thought were my friends, but we both know how that turned out."

He peered at her, noticing her defenses fall, "How's everything been, really?"

Her fingers traced the edge of her glass, the cool wine sweating onto her fingertips. She had been careful until now.

She had masterfully been able to steer the conversations and questions away from *that* topic. But here she was, sitting across from Wes, so patient and understanding that she couldn't find a reason to bottle it up inside anymore.

"One of my good friends had an affair with my husband," she said. "They had been exes without me knowing, so I'm sure it had been going on our whole relationship. I was just too stupid to see it," she explained.

Charlotte froze immediately, her pulse thundering in her ears. But he was quiet, and a stillness hung between them. Her cheeks burned as she got the sudden urge to crawl into herself. Instead, she forced herself to breathe, to calm the panic that had risen in her chest.

"That must've been so painful," he said warmly, leaning forward just slightly.

His tender stare melted the shame she felt, her embarrassment sliding away. It was suddenly not as overwhelming as it once was. The thought of her ex-husband's betrayal wasn't so threatening anymore. He listened, without judgement, as she confessed to him her truth. She didn't feel as small as she did before, in what seemed like a whole other life.

"Yeah, it was," she breathed, her gaze steady now.

Wes gave her a small nod, the corners of his mouth lifting slightly. He didn't rush to say anything or try to fix her brokenness; he simply sat in the weight of it with her. Somehow, it was exactly what she needed. For the first time in a long time, she wasn't afraid of speaking her truth.

The cotton candy sky above them created an amber hue of nostalgia for Charlotte. She used to love New England summers as a child and couldn't believe she hadn't been back since then. Memories of her and her grandmother shucking corn on the back porch while her grandfather brought home the biggest lobsters her little eyes had ever seen. Sometimes, if she went down to the harbor with him, he would playfully torment her by placing the large brown paper bag filled with lobsters next to her on the car ride home. She would pretend to be brave as she heard their claws clattering against one another, trying to climb to the top. When she would muster up the courage, she would carefully peer inside the crinkly bag, praying they were near the bottom and not trying to escape. Her grandfather would laugh at her uncertainty, assuring her they could not get out. She would hesitantly giggle as they drove on, trying to hide her fear of being pinched by one of their large claws.

Asher never had any desire to leave Washington, but her constant hints of a desire to live anywhere else went unnoticed by him, countless times. She was reminded how unseen she was and how isolating that felt. At that moment, she wished she had fought for her wants and desires instead of brushing them aside. It struck her that it may have been easier to follow his path, but she was now realizing how much it had affected her confidence. Knowing this earlier would have never saved her marriage, but at least she was currently learning from that mistake.

She and Wes chatted and drank their beverages as the night wound down. People were leaving with their canvas, and the music slowly diminished. They glanced at each other, laughing as Susan noticed their attentiveness towards each other, a smile sweeping across her face.

Boom.

Charlotte's eyes were fixed on the sky, watching the fireworks explode in a burst of color and light, but his gaze never left her.

Chapter 14

Newport, Rhode Island, Present Day: Wes & Charlotte

"Well, I'd call that a success," Wes said, throwing away empty cups that had fallen on the grass.

"I have to agree with you," a tipsy Susan smirked as she sank into a chair.

The backyard was a bit of a mess. Red, white, and blue streamers littered the lawn, echoes of a good time now fading into the stillness of the evening.

"I am happy to report that all works of art were bid on and purchased," Charlotte announced, counting the wad of money in her hands.

"How much?" Susan asked.

"A little over $4,000," Charlotte beamed.

"Fabulous," Susan clapped.

Charlotte could hear distant firecrackers as a soft, cool wind rustled the paper plates and napkins that were strewn across the tables.

Wes took a sip of his drink and, with wide eyes, watched Charlotte and Susan with a mixture of disbelief and appreciation. This stranger from Seattle had walked into their lives, bringing sparks of happiness wherever she went. She wasn't looking for any applause or grand gesture; she acted on the goodness of her heart with no ulterior motive. Her small but significant act of kindness acted as a quiet ripple in the still waters of the day.

"I have to hand it to you guys, it was a great party. Grandma, Pop would be proud," Wes said, lifting his glass before taking a sip.

A soft smile played on Susan's lips as she watched her grandson, now a grown man. He had always been a quiet boy, one who did not seek any attention from others. She remembered his tiny hands clinging to the edge of her skirt as he learned to walk, and she could never forget the sound of his infectious giggles as he watched their family dog chase the chickens that once skittered across their yard. Her eyes softened as she smiled, as if the memory was a friend she'd just welcomed back after a long trip away. She sat with a quiet admiration for him and who he had become.

***

Seattle, Washington, Two Years Prior

Charlotte sat alone one evening at the kitchen table, the cold light of the evening casting a pale glow on her face. The soft, steady patter of raindrops against the window washed away any doubt. Her fingers drummed the wooden surface, her eyes darting to the clock. She knew Asher should be home soon, her pulse quickening with anticipation of his arrival.

She heard the keys clang as they dangled on the doorknob, his boots stomping on the front porch. The door opened, and with a quick flick of her hand, she wiped a single tear away.

"We need to talk," she said.

Asher paused, unsure how to reply. He set his things

down as he trudged into the kitchen, setting his keys down on the counter.

"Me too," he said, taking a seat.

With his hands loosely clasped in front of him, he took a seat across from her. She looked at him directly, her eyes no longer wavering as they used to.

"I want a divorce," she said. Charlotte's lips trembled, but she held her ground. She could see Asher's mind reeling. He stared blankly back at her, as if trying to decode her words. His face shifted to confusion and then disbelief.

"What? No...we can come back from this," he mumbled, a quiet sadness tightening his voice.

" We haven't been fine for a long time," she said, crossing her arms as if to shield herself from the anger she could see welling up inside his chest. "I've spent so long trying to convince myself that we could make this work, but we are beyond repair."

"Charlotte, this can't be what you want," he said, his skin pale as a ghost. The air was thick with unspoken tension that Charlotte was ready to be rid of.

Her eyes softened, but she didn't flinch.

Asher swallowed hard, his lips tightening into a straight line.

"I'm done," she said, with a strengthened voice.

Asher nodded slowly, blinking back a hint of tears, "I guess I knew in the back of my mind that this would happen, but I hoped it wouldn't."

Charlotte offered him a small smile as the rain outside blustered against the window. Sometimes the hardest thing isn't leaving, it's accepting that you have to.

***

Newport, Rhode Island, Present Day: Wes & Charlotte

Charlotte let the trash can lid by the street crash as it closed, containing the remnants of a fun Fourth of July. She walked back inside and went upstairs for a quick shower. She changed into cotton shorts and a strappy tank top, pulling her wet hair back into a bun on top of her head.

Wes's voice was sharp but strained, "No, I don't think that is a good idea. You expect me to just go along with everything, and that's not what I want to do."

Charlotte stiffened, hesitating at the top of the stairs. She wasn't intending on eavesdropping, but the anger in Wes's voice stopped her in her tracks.

"Yes, Emily. Charlotte is staying with my grandmother, but only until she figures something out," he explained.

Charlotte's heart started pounding in her chest. Her fingers tightened around the railing as she leaned slightly forward, trying to hear the rest of his private conversation.

"I don't think it's that big of a deal. Plus, I'm telling you *now*," he said, clicking the speakerphone button on his phone to hear his fiancée more clearly.

Charlotte could hear the shrillness in Emily's voice, "So now Charlotte gets a free pass? You're letting her stay with your family while I'm here in Martha's Vineyard planning our wedding alone? That's for sure the beginning of a great marriage."

Charlotte's stomach began to twist as she listened in.

"Emily, I told you, nothing is going on between us. Charlotte needs a place to stay, and this is all just temporary."

Charlotte pressed her back up against the wall to steady herself as her thoughts spiraled. Here she was in the middle of their argument, listening as a wall of resentment built between them brick by brick. Unfortunately, Charlotte felt like the glue holding it all together.

"You think it's just temporary?" she huffed. "I'm here planning our *future* while you're playing house with another woman! I'm not okay with this. You shouldn't have let this happen!"

Charlotte winced, her fingers gripping the railing even harder. She couldn't move. If she went downstairs now, she would be interrupting a conversation that wasn't meant for her. A part of her wanted to pick up her things and head back to the hotel, but another part of her wanted to hear Wes defend his grandmother's choice. If she were being honest, she wanted to hear him defend her as well. It wasn't *his* decision, after all. That was the part Emily could not let go of.

"I didn't think this would bother you. My grandmother made the offer, who am I to tell her what to do?" he said.

"This is a huge problem. I want her out of your grandmother's house!" Emily's voice crackled under the weight of her frustration.

Wes sighed and spoke with a quiet determination, "It is only a problem if you let it be, Emily. Charlotte is doing amazing things for my grandmother. She isn't so lonely anymore, and I refuse to take that away from her because it makes *you* uncomfortable," he explained.

Charlotte looked up in surprise. The slight vulnerability that usually clung to Wes had now been replaced by something fierce, protection. Something warmed and curled in Charlotte's chest.

"If you still want this wedding to happen, you will fix this!" Emily demanded, followed by a click to end the call.

Charlotte could feel Emily's heavy words resting on her chest. Charlotte hadn't asked for this. She hadn't wanted to become a complication in anyone's life. But somehow, she had. The silence in the hallway was suffocating as an ache pulled her chest inward. She wanted to slip back into the shadows of her room, unnoticed. She didn't want him to know she had been listening, but she also couldn't escape the feeling that she had been a part of something she didn't understand.

"Charlotte?" he said, looking up at her from the bottom of the stairs.

Charlotte's senses shot back as though her mind was elsewhere. She hadn't even noticed him walk into the family room.

"Hey," she said.

"Do you want a nightcap? Out on the deck?" he asked.

She wasn't sure if he knew she had just heard the whole argument between him and his fiancée...about her.

"Sure," she said, padding down the stairs.

The evening sky was drenched with violet, streaks of sunlight slipping quickly behind the horizon. Cicadas filled the air with their rhythmic hum as fireflies flickered like stars, weaving in and out of the trees before them. They chatted like old friends, two glasses of half-finished wine between them. Charlotte leaned back in her chair, her legs tucked underneath her. Her glassy gaze shifted to Wes. His cheeks were flushed from the wine, his eyes more animated than usual. His shirt sleeves were rolled up to his elbow, a carelessness to his appearance that made him even more appealing to the eye. Her eyes slowly traced his tattoos curling around his forearms.

"You see those fireflies?" he asked. " They're glowing like they know something we don't."

Charlotte smiled, amused by his tipsy observation.

"Maybe they're just trying to distract you from being serious all the time," she said.

Wes laughed, but not one that could be described as carefree. This laugh was weighted more, a bit melancholy. His eyes drifted from the fireflies to Charlotte, and for a moment, he seemed to lose focus, his eyes lingering a bit longer than necessary.

"Those tattoos," she pointed. "What's the meaning behind them?"

"Now that's a good question," he said, placing his wine glass down. He rolled up his shirt sleeves some more, exposing more of the black ink and the toned muscle underneath them. Charlotte caught her breath as he did this, her mind racing.

"They all represent something different," he said, pointing to his right arm. "This sleeve represents my childhood. The boat and the octopus are one of my favorite memories. As a kid, I used to go boating with my grandfather all the time. One time, as we were pulling the lobster net in, a huge red octopus was stuck to the net. I was kind of scared by it, but my grandfather loved it. He explained everything there was to know about them. All that shading you see that moves from darker to light? That represents time passing. But the boat is an actual replica of my grandfather's."

"It's impressive," she said. "Did it hurt?"

"Oh, like hell," he laughed.

As he continued to talk about the other sleeve on his opposite arm, Charlotte couldn't resist what it would feel like to be engulfed by him. She pictured him picking her up and placing her on the bed that lay untouched a few feet away from them. She thought of how he would slide off his shirt, exposing his broad chest and shoulders as she lay defenseless under his body. She would move her fingers across his tattoos as he kissed her so tenderly.

"Do you have any?" he asked, interrupting her racy thoughts.

"I have one," she said, showing the small butterfly on the inside of her ankle.

"What does that represent?" he asked.

"It's a long story," she said.

As Charlotte chuckled, her eyes lit up with effortless charm. Wes found himself tracing the curve of her smile, the sound of her laugh warming the space between them.

"I wish I could be more like you," he said. "You're just...you."

Charlotte blinked, caught off guard by the unexpected compliment. There was something in the way that he said it, like a truth he's just now realizing for the first time.

"What do you mean?" she asked.

Wes leaned back in his chair, his shoulders softening. The wine drenched his words with sweetness, "You don't try to impress people, you just be who you are. I've been pretending for so long, you know? Like I've got this *thing* figured out. But you? You don't even have to try."

Charlotte's pulse quickened. She wasn't sure if it was

his words or the wine that were making her knees weak. His voice was soothing.

"Wes, I hate to break it to you, but I don't have anything figured out."

He leaned forward, his eyes dark with something she couldn't quite place. It was as if he was trying to let down every wall that had built up between them.

"What if it was you and me?" he whispered, barely audible.

Charlotte's voice caught in her throat. She forced herself to look away, her eyes fixated on the fireflies. She wished the gentle glow of their bodies could offer her a warm reprieve from this moment. A moment she wasn't sure she was ready for.

"Wes. You've made decisions, big ones. You have Emily," she said.

Wes's smile faltered, a pang of regret flickering in his eyes, as if he were suddenly feeling the weight of his words.

"I think we've had a lot to drink and it's time to turn in," she said.

"I didn't mean to make this weird," he said. "I'm sorry."

Charlotte's heart ached at the apology. She could tell he wasn't upset at what he said, but for the implication, for what it means. The feelings between them were dangerous and complicated. It was in both of their best interests to ignore them.

"You make it so hard to pretend," he said.

Wes' eyes darkened, a shadow crossing over his face. His glass of wine was forgotten in his hand as he looked out into the night. Charlotte let the silence between them thicken, a bittersweet feeling pulling at her chest. He confirmed their attraction toward one another, which, in a way, validated her own feelings. She wasn't just imagining his lingering stares or his flirty disposition. There was something about him that she wasn't ready to let go of yet, and neither was he.

Chapter 15

The sun dipped below the horizon as Wes stood at the edge of the cliffs overlooking Newport's rugged coastline. His hands were stuffed into his pockets, his eyes lost in the shifting waves below.

His phone buzzed in his pocket, another reminder about his upcoming wedding plans. But Wes didn't reach for it. He knew what his fiancée would be saying. She was trying to finalize menus, the flowers, and invitations. It was all right there, staring him in the face. A future he couldn't seem to escape from, even if he wanted to.

It wasn't that he didn't care about Emily; he did. She was safe and predictable, something he needed growing up, that is, until he met Charlotte.

God, Charley.

Her face, her laugh, the way she made him feel alive in a way he hadn't felt in years. A part of him hated that. Hated how effortlessly she had stepped into his life, as if she was always meant to be there. He hated how easy it was to talk to her, how she made him forget the knot of guilt that had been twisting in his stomach since their first conversation.

His chest churned at the thought of her, how he wasn't supposed to feel this way about her. It was supposed to be

Emily. Not when he had a life laid out in front of him, a future he had spent years shaping. A future that was comfortable, with in-laws who had money and a secure legacy to fall into.

But what if that legacy was already suffocating him? What is that future wasn't enough?

Wes closed his eyes as he pinched the bridge of his nose, drawing in a slow breath. Emily was predictable, yes, but that wasn't what had been eating away at his peace. It was the idea of spending the rest of his life in a box, checking things off her list. He wasn't sure he wanted that life anymore. Not really.

Charlotte's smile filled the forefront of his mind, the fire in her eyes. She wasn't easy, and he wasn't sure she fit inside his neat little life. But maybe that was exactly why he couldn't stop thinking about her. She was the wild card, the unknown.

His mind spiraled. He thought of the demons he'd spent years trying to bury, trying to ignore. The fear of being judged for cutting himself free. The shame of not living up to everyone's expectations had kept him up, night after night. The tangled mess of emotions in his mind that he couldn't quite undo had all come to a head. He placed a hand on his chest as the crashing waves below him roared. His heart raced, sending cool chills up his arms. He closed his eyes as he let the uneasy feeling take over, numbing any other feeling he had wanted to feel. His eyelids fluttered open, a bead of sweat trickling down his temple.

Emily had never seen him like this before, so wrecked with the unknown. She hadn't asked how any of this affected him. The gnawing feeling inside him grew stronger. He shifted his gaze to the horizon, anything to allow this feeling to pass. He didn't know how to walk away from a life that was already mapped out for him. He didn't know how to walk away from Emily. He'd known her his whole life. Their parents had been friends since they were babies.

He had to decide. Soon. Before he lost everything he was too afraid to let go of. He turned away from the edge of the cliffs, pulling his phone out of his pocket. A message from his fiancée blinked on the screen: *"Call me. We need to discuss a few things, love you."*

But Wes wasn't thinking about her, about their wedding. He thought of Charley, the freedom she brought into his life. She wasn't demanding his time, or anything for that matter. She had no idea of the way she made him question everything he'd settled for. Or did she?

He turned his head, looking out into the ocean once again. For the first time in years, the horizon had felt wide open. But that freedom came with a weight. A choice he didn't know how to make. He was caught between what was safe and what could be something more.

And that choice terrified him.

***

Newport, Rhode Island, Present Day: Charlotte

"Do you need more cream and sugar?" Susan asked, watching Charlotte pour her second cup of coffee.

"Yes please," she said, grabbing a spoon.

"Here," Susan said, passing the sugar container. "If it doesn't taste like dessert if it's not perfect enough," she laughed.

"I agree," Charlotte said. "Hey, how about we go for a drive today? Ocean Drive?"

Susan looked up from her newspaper, crinkling its center.

"It might be nice to get out of the house," Charlotte said.

"I would like that very much," Susan said. "Ten minutes?"

"Let me go upstairs to change."

Minutes later, they stepped outside, and Susan handed Charlotte her car keys.

"I'd rather you drive," she instructed. "My eyes just aren't what they used to be."

"Okay," Charlotte said, dangling the keys in her hand. "You know, I don't think I've ever seen your car."

The garage door slowly creaked open, its hinges barely holding on. However, when she first noticed Susan's antique, she nearly gasped.

"Is that an old Jaguar?" she uttered, its candy-red apple color shining in the sunlight.

"Yes, an '85 Cabriolet." She smiled. "It was my father's, and he passed it down to me."

"It's beautiful," Charlotte gushed. "I'm not a car person, but this is amazing."

"The top goes down," Susan said. "It's still warm and sunny, so I do suggest riding with it down today. You know, to get the full effect," she said, her smile widening.

Charlotte walked toward the car, placing a hand on the trunk.

"We used to ride it all around town," Susan explained.

"I loved to be seen in it. My friends thought it was the coolest thing."

"I bet," Charlotte replied. "Are you sure it's okay for me to drive?"

"Of course, it's a car, it's supposed to be driven. Plus, I can't remember the last time it has seen the road. I mean, I walk everywhere around here."

"Alright," Charlotte said. "Let's go."

As they both stepped into the car, Charlotte's nose was instantly met with the smell of old leather and lingering cigarette smoke.

"My dad used to smoke," she said. "I swear, whenever I miss him, I just sit in here."

Charlotte smiled and started up the car. Its engine purred, causing Susan to burst into laughter.

"There she is," Susan exclaimed, a bigger smile could never adorn her face.

Charlotte cautiously backed the car out of the driveway and started down the street. She slowly turned onto Bellevue Avenue, mesmerized by the faces of the historic mansions that were perched behind rod iron gates. The red tulips that lined the sidewalks swayed lightly as the wind breathed life into their petals. The air smelled of sea salt and sweetness, the kind of aroma that you wished were contained in a candle.

"Just that way, dear," Susan smiled, pointing forward. "Take a right."

Charlotte turned to the right, as instructed. What unfolded in front of them should have been a painting. The tall sea grass swayed as the rocky banks of the ocean welcomed crashing waves onto the shore. The robin egg blue sky was spotless, as pristine as its glossy water beneath it. Charlotte's smile could not be denied. Susan looked over at her, their hair moving every which way.

"Isn't this a treat?" Susan giggled.

"This is unreal," Charlotte said, driving onward, feeling as free as she ever had before.

"Have you been to Castle Hill before?" Susan asked.

"Wes took me there, to the lighthouse," Charlotte said. "We had brunch afterward. It was beautiful."

"I want to take you to another little spot. Somewhere that is special to me."

Susan pointed and alerted her right before the turn, excitement bubbling out of her chest.

As they rounded the corner, the car climbed to the top of a small hill. Charlotte parked, and both women sprang out of the car.

"I want to show you this overlook," Susan said. "It's just this way."

Susan took the lead down a narrow dirt path that wound through trees and brush. As they walked, Susan was quiet, paying special attention to where she was stepping.

"How are you doing?" Charlotte asked.

"I'm fine," Susan replied.

Charlotte's eyes marveled at the dappled light that played peekaboo with her behind the gently swaying trees. Hidden birds were nestled in the brush, quickly jumping from branch to branch, playing tag with one another. After a few minutes, the trail they were on began to open up, and the dirt was quickly replaced with bright green grass. Susan's footsteps quickened to match her excitement.

"Now this," she said. "Is the best view."

The hill they were perched on revealed waves that gushed against the shore, dousing the rocky cliffs below in white froth. Sunbeams surfed atop the tide, their cylinders of light effortlessly skimmed across the sea. The lighthouse stood as a guardian, monitoring the sailboats that cleaved through the water.

"Wow," Charlotte said.

"I know," Susan said. "Push down the need to talk, just soak it all in."

The women stood in silence, breathing in the essence of peace the ocean bestowed on them. They welcomed the silent moments of tranquility, allowing them to cleanse their souls. The isolation Charlotte had felt, gripped so tightly on her heart, began to fall away again. The ocean had a way of rinsing her of her past.

"Come, follow me, just this way," Susan said.

Moments later, Susan bent down to take a seat on a large rock, jutting into the water, small waves lapping against it.

"You okay? Charlotte asked.

"Yeah, just tired," Susan said.

"Well, just relax," Charlotte said.

"I'll rest when I'm dead," she shot back.

Susan's flippant comment caused Charlotte to howl in laughter; her guffawing could be heard across the bay.

"You are something else," Charlotte said.

"When you're my age, everything is light and fun. I wish I could have told my younger self that everything wasn't so serious."

Charlotte turned to listen.

"Looking back, there were so many people and situations that did not deserve so much of my energy. However, there were some I wish I had given more energy to."

"Like what?" Charlotte asked.

"Oh, you wouldn't want to hear a sappy story, would you?"

"Of course, I would."

Susan's memory ignited a flame deep within her that hadn't been lit in years.

"After college, I came home to live with my parents for the summer. You know, broke and clueless," she explained.

Charlotte leaned in towards Susan.

"I had fallen in love with this boy from high school, but we had separated before I left for college. Well, fast forward four years, I was walking through the grocery store trying to find various things for my mother, and as I was lifting to grab a box of baking soda, I could feel someone watching me."

"And?" Charlotte asked.

"Well, I looked down the aisle, and that same boy walked towards me as a man. Aisle number six. He had the same kind eyes as before and helped me find the rest of the groceries my mother needed. We talked the entire time and met up a few times after that."

"And?" Charlotte repeated.

"We spent the summer together, running around town and reminiscing," Susan giggled. "We would steal that car way past midnight and drive to the beach."

"The Cabriolet?" Charlotte asked.

"Yes!" she said. "We would put the top down and drive up and down the Pell Bridge and stare up at the stars. Gosh, we thought it would never end. "

"Why did it end?" Charlotte asked.

"He went off to California to work with his uncle in Napa. He promised he would return, but he never did. After two years, I gave up and moved to Boston to start my own life."

"He never called you?" Charlotte asked.

"Honey, there were no cell phones back then," she said. "He never wrote either. Not a single letter."

Charlotte could see the depth of sorrow in Susan's eyes.

"All was well, eventually. I met my husband, and we got married, had our kids, and moved back here. And you know what? Life moved right along."

"What was his name?" Charlotte asked.

"Oh, that ship has sailed," She waved off Charlotte's clear intentions.

"Oh, come on, I'm sure we could find something. Everyone has either a Facebook or an Instagram page nowadays."

"Not me," Susan said.

"Well, you may be the only one."

Charlotte watched as Susan fell silent, her eyes watching the waves in the distance, her heart swelling with the tide.

"August," she whispered. "His name was August Mansfield."

Charlotte whipped out her phone and typed his name

into Facebook search.

"Is this him?" Charlotte asked, moments later. She turned her phone to Susan, and as soon as her eyes settled onto his, her eyes became misted with her billowing emotions.

"Yes," she uttered. "Oh, I'd remember that smile anywhere."

Charlotte's smile laid flat as she swiped up and down his Facebook page.

Susan sat back as if to already knew what Charlotte was going to say next.

"He died years ago," Charlotte said. "What makes it worse is that he lived here."

"He lived here?" Susan asked.

"Yes, he lived in Jamestown."

Susan didn't speak; her eyes shifted back to the water as her spine became rigid.

"Jamestown isn't that far from here," she muttered.

"What if he moved back here for you?" Charlotte said.

Susan's eyes sank to the bottom of Narragansett Bay, regret tugging at her heart as if it were an anchor.

"I was in Boston," she said.

Charlotte clicked her phone off and put it back into her jeans pocket.

Susan's demeanor became complacent.

"It wasn't written in our story, dear."

"It's not fair," Charlotte said.

"Not a lot is fair," Susan said. "Things happen for reasons we may never be able to answer," Susan said. "You can't control everything."

Charlotte crossed her legs and rested her intertwined

hands on her knee. She never thought of her life as delicate as it truly was.

"I have an idea," Charlotte sat up. "Come with me!"

In the old car that held so many memories deep within its leather seats, Charlotte drove Susan across the Pell Bridge and back, just as Susan and August did many years before. With the top lowered, the wind leapt from the bay, sweeping the memory of August against Susan's cheeks, her smile as wide as the sea below them.

***

Seattle, Washington, Two Years Prior: Charlotte

After asking her husband for a divorce, Asher left Seattle to go visit his family in Arizona. She was sure he would tell his parents of the demise of their marriage and wondered how they would take the news. So far, she had been de-friended on social media by his close friends and cousins.

She knew she couldn't stay in the empty house all day, so instead, she grabbed her old tennis shoes and a jacket and slipped them on. She plucked her journal from her purse and headed out the door. There was a small trail that she followed, easy and short, but it led to the most magnificent view of Puget Sound. She hadn't visited there in a while and figured it was time. As her feet hit the solid ground of the path, her eyes widened in amazement. The golden trails of light flickered from one fir tree to the next, accentuating its darkened green branches. She looked ahead and began to smell the ocean. She loved the Pacific Northwest; it had a way of reenergizing her senses.

The trail became smaller, and a clearing slowly came

into view. The ocean revealed itself, its waves drifting past Bainbridge Island. There was a rock that jutted out of the earth, the most perfect bench. She took a seat and drew in a deep breath. Her soul so desperately needed this. She unfastened the leather strings that bound her precious words together and began to write. Her innermost thoughts and feelings now found solace in the pages of her journal. Her mind had no trouble emptying the toxins from her life over the last few months. Her pen rolled feverishly onto the page as she freed herself from the trenches that had been the whirlwind of her life. She knew she couldn't live this way any longer. Trapped in a loveless marriage where trust had been shattered. Her husband loved another, her best friend at that. The betrayal she felt rattled itself inside her chest, clenching her heart. At that moment, she decided she could not see past it. She could not let it go.

She knew deep within her heart that she needed to free herself from Asher and Seattle. If she were being honest, she had felt her love for him slip away longer than she wanted to admit. She truly loved him at an earlier time in her life, but seeing how he reacted when she needed him the most let her down, time after time. Wasting her life waiting on someone to be the person they would never be would satisfy her. The sadness that overwhelmed her slowly turned into hope. She knew she couldn't stay in Seattle; she had to start fresh somewhere else. Somewhere she didn't know anybody, and no one had preconceived notions about her. The possibility of meeting someone to trust with her heart was there, but that wouldn't be her sole focus. She knew that to ever make that happen in the future, she needed to work on herself first. Dive deeper into the person she was now becoming. That an energy shift would allow her to realize she was evolving. Becoming a stronger version of herself was her sole purpose now. This transition in her life was a gradual transformation of who she was supposed to always become, an opportunity some might never have. She felt empowered and proud of herself.

Her butterfly era had begun.

***

Newport, Rhode Island, Present Day: Wes

Eight long hours later, Wes finally left the hospital. Images of his patient's worried family members were on his mind. The surgery he performed went longer than expected and was sprinkled with a few complications that had popped up unexpectedly. His ears were throbbing where the elastic of the mask had been, causing them to be raw to the touch. He winced as he got into his car and started the short drive to his grandmother's house.

As he walked inside, a smile plastered itself onto his face. Music blared from the kitchen, and as he walked in and made his way through the hallway, both Susan's and Charlotte's laughter echoed throughout the house.

"Add more flour!" Charlotte laughed. "The dough is so sticky."

"I'm trying," Susan wheezed as she laughed uncontrollably.

"It's sourdough bread, not expensive china," she playfully yelled over the music.

"What is so special about this bread?" Susan asked.

"Everyone's doing it!" she said. "It's all over social

media."

"Why are *we* doing it?" Susan repeated.

"What else do we have going on?" she asked.

They both heard a crack on the floor and looked up, covered from head to toe in flour.

"Well, you're finally home," Susan said, welcoming her grandson and turning down the music.

"I need to run upstairs and shower before I come near you two. I just wanted to see what the commotion was all about," he said.

"Well, we're in no shape to come near you either," she teased, looking at Charlotte. Flour had kissed her nose and covered her matching apron.

Wes beamed, looking at Charlotte through his lashes.

As he turned and walked up the stairs, he took off his shirt. Sweat dripped down his back, and he felt like he had run a marathon. Once in his room, he began to disrobe, unraveling the chaos from his day. His worries melted away as the hot water slid down his skin. He raised his hands to his head, wiping away the water that had collected there. The realization of how strenuous his shift had been had finally sunk in. His brain rattled on as he showered, going through the surgery in his mind, as if it were a broken record.

***

Newport, Rhode Island, Present Day: Charlotte

Thirty minutes later, Charlotte watched as Wes descended the stairs, the old wood announcing his presence. His gray jogger sweatpants accentuated his strong calves and toned thighs. His navy blue t-shirt showed off his robust chest, and the remnants of his shower still sparkled on the tips of his hair. She almost couldn't pry her eyes off him. Susan had the remote, feverishly clicking through channels to find a good show.

"You know you can just watch Netflix, Grandma," Wes said. Susan looked up at him, annoyed, with some remnants of flour still on her clothes.

"They don't have my show, it's so frustrating," she said.

The moment snapped, and Charlotte quickly looked away as she realized she was staring at Wes a little too intently. She quickly got up to refill her empty wine glass. He quietly followed behind, his eyes trailing her petite body.

"Let me help you," he smiled, his dimples coming to life as the burgundy wine effortlessly slipped into her glass.

"You need one too," she said. "You had an extra-long shift."

"You're not wrong," he sighed, grabbing another glass and pouring one for himself.

"Was it bad?" she asked, taking a seat across from him on the island.

"I had a difficult surgery today," he said. "It was challenging, but I got myself and the patient through it. What did you two do today?"

Charlotte leaned forward, practically glowing.

"We took the Cabriolet down Ocean Drive, and it was the most perfect day," she said.

Wes watched her with a warm appreciation. The way her eyes lit up when she talked pulled him into her world. *She was magic,* he thought.

"You've driven it, right?" she asked.

Wes was so mesmerized by her that he didn't notice she had finished talking.

"She let you drive that old car?" he asked.

"You haven't?" she asked again, taking a sip of her wine.

"No, I've never been allowed."

"Oh," she chuckled.

After a few moments, Susan walked in, announcing her bedtime.

"Night, Grandma," he said, gently placing a kiss on the top of her head.

Charlotte smiled as Susan turned on her heels, walking up the steps to her bedroom.

"Just us," Wes said.

"Do you wanna make a fire outside?" Charlotte asked, "If you're too tired, I understand."

"No, let's do it. I'm off tomorrow anyway, so I'll be able to sleep in."

The two grabbed their wine glasses and headed down the stairs to the backyard. Wes grabbed four pieces of firewood as Charlotte nestled into her chair, placing a cozy cashmere blanket in her lap. The night air was crisp as a chilly breeze tousled her hair. A circle of soft, golden light radiated around the fire as Wes threw the match into the grass. The embers cast gentle flickers over their faces as they both watched the fire emerge.

"So," he sighed, taking a seat next to her.

"So," Charlotte said. Her knees to her chest, leaning closer toward the fire.

Wes laughed.

"What?" she asked, the flames reflecting in her eyes.

"Do you ever just wonder how we got here?" he asked, his voice soft as the crackling fire filled the pause between them.

"I could say the same thing. You're not exactly who I pictured I'd be spending my Friday night with," she said, a smile tugging at her lips.

We tilted his head, teasing her with a playful smirk. "Oh? Who did you think you'd be spending it with?"

"I don't know...someone, anyone else," she teased.

The fire crackled louder, casting fleeting shadows against the back of Susan's house. Without a word, he reached for his glass, taking a sip.

"You know," he said. "This is way better than the movie I had in mind."

She sipped her wine, glancing sideways at him.

They fell into a comfortable silence, both of their chins facing upward toward the stars. The weight of the night between them felt like it belonged to nobody else. The world outside their intimate circle of warmth felt distant, as if time had slowed. Allowing them to just...be.

"I'm glad I'm here with you, though," Charlotte said, "And Susan."

Wes's hand found hers, as if being pulled by some unrecognizable force. Their fingers intertwined naturally, and her thumb traced the back of his hand so naturally.

The only thing that existed was this soft, shared moment between them, and the realization that things had changed between them. They both could not deny the shift in the air that occurred when their fingers touched, and for once, neither of them wanted to leave.

The sky was a canvas of stars as the crickets filled the silence around them. Wes slowly dropped her hand, "I never thought I'd be sitting here with you, like this."

She met his gaze, her heart racing. Her expression stayed calm yet understanding.

"I know," she replied warmly. "I never imagined this either. But maybe we're not meant to follow the paths we've been given. Maybe we're meant to choose our own."

There was a flicker of something in his eyes, of both admiration and fear. Despite the heaviness of the situation, he couldn't deny her words. His eyes softened as he reached out slowly, as if testing the waters again. His hand, warm and sure, hovered above hers. She didn't hesitate as her small and delicate hands slipped back into his. The touch was simple yet profound. All of the tensions and complications faded away, if only for the moment.

The weight of his fiancée's absence hung heavily between them now, yet nobody said a word of it. Neither of them wanted to. What could they say that hadn't already been said in their hearts?

His thumb brushed her knuckles, a silent apology for the forbidden nature of their bond.

"You're so brave," she whispered, not wanting to shatter the moment between them.

"I'm not brave," he said. "I'm just following my heart."

For a moment, nobody moved. No words could capture the turbulent feelings coiling in the air around them. The world would not approve. The rules were set against them, and yet, in this small moment beneath the stars, none of that mattered.

Their fingers tightened, a small act of defiance against all of the things they couldn't change. They didn't speak of the future or any plans of changing their paths, just two people soaking in what was and could be.

For once, it felt like they were exactly where they were supposed to be.

Chapter 16

Newport, Rhode Island, Present Day: Charlotte

"Charlotte?" Susan yelled up the stairs.

"On my way down!" she yelled back, pulling on her bathrobe and quickly descending the stairs, her thoughts of the night before tucked away in her memories.

"Want any bacon?" Susan asked as Charlotte looked at Wes behind the stove.

"Sure," she said, taking a seat behind the island.

"Coffee?" Wes asked, sliding her a mug.

"Yes, please," she said.

"So did you two go right to bed last night?" Susan prodded.

"We started a fire and hung out for a bit," Wes said, shooting a grin at Charlotte as the bacon sizzled in the pan in front of him.

Susan speculated but didn't ask any further questions.

"Wes almost fell asleep in his chair, so we came back in shortly after that," Charlotte said.

"You did?" Susan asked.

Wes playfully rolled his eyes with confirmation.

"Charlotte, would you like to go on a walk with me after breakfast?" Wes asked.

"Sure," Charlotte said, taking a long chug of her coffee.

Susan's eyes darted from Wes to Charlotte.

"Without me?" Susan asked.

"I mean, you can come," Wes offered.

"I'm just kidding, I want to call my friend and catch up," Susan said.

The three of them finished breakfast, laughing from time to time.

"Ready?" Wes asked, taking everybody's plates to the sink.

"Yeah, let me go upstairs to change, and I'll be ready."

"Sounds good," Wes said, placing everything in the dishwasher.

After ten minutes, Charlotte met Wes out front. He was tying his shoes as she slowly walked down the steps.

"Was this your way of getting me alone?" she asked.

"Maybe," he said, standing up straight.

As they started to walk down Thames Street towards the Wharf, Charlotte placed her hands in her pockets as Wes nervously paced next to her. A slight breeze sent a chill down her spine, her back stiffening. She knew they had to talk about what had happened the night before, what it now meant. Maybe it wasn't anything, maybe it was his desperation to hang onto something exciting in his world that felt like it was falling apart. As quickly as she wanted to shove those feelings of doubt out of her mind, images of the night before controlled her thoughts now. She remembered how powerful he felt as his hands wrapped around hers, as if she were a feather, so soft and tender.

"You have a fiancée, Wes," Charlotte blurted out, without a plan.

The Wharf was shrouded in thick, heavy fog. The kind that muffled sound and gave everything a sense of isolation. The water below them on the dock was dark and restless, the air damp and salty, clinging to their clothes. A grayness hung over them like a veil while the storm between them brewed, as if their time and consequences were held in limbo.

Wes stood at the edge of the wooden dock, his back to Charlotte, his hands shoved deep into his pockets. He didn't respond as the waves lapped around them. Charlotte stood in place, watching the dense mist swirl around the docked boats close by. As her hair was being disheveled by the wind, her eyes were fixated on him. She had always been able to read him, even behind his well-crafted walls.

"Why did you ask me to come here?" she asked softly, her voice almost lost in the fog. "What is it that you want from me?"

Her words hit him like a cold slap, forcing him to turn and face her. She was standing before him, looking impossibly beautiful, even in the dreary morning light. He slowly stepped toward her.

"I need you to understand something," he began. "I can't keep doing this, I can't keep pretending that what I have with Emily is enough."

Charlotte blinked, a flicker of confusion swept across her face.

He shook his head, frustration flaring in his chest, "I'm leaving her."

The fog seemed to thicken, as if the world were holding them in place.

"What do you mean? You're engaged. You're about to

marry her," she trailed off.

"I can't," he interrupted. "I can't do it. I thought I was supposed to be with her, but since you've come here, I've realized that she may not be where my story ends."

He paused, his eyes searching hers for some kind of understanding. Her pain was evident by the way her lips pursed together. The wind swirled around them, the fog becoming denser between them. The distant seagulls echoed hollowly across the water.

"I don't want to hurt you," taking another step towards her. His breath caught in his throat as he watched her trembling slightly. Whether it was the chillness of the breeze or something deeper, he couldn't tell. "But I can't keep pretending this between us isn't real."

He looked at her as if she were the only thing that mattered in the world, "I can't live with myself anymore, not if it means living a life that's a lie."

She met his gaze, her eyes sharp and searching for the words, any words that could make sense of their situation. She opened her lips to speak, but nothing emerged.

His throat tightened, "I can't go back to her. I can't go back to a life that isn't honest."

She could see the weight of his decision, the years of lies and guilt, crashing down before him. That didn't make it any less complicated.

"You're making a huge mistake," she muttered. Her words came out broken and shattered. "You're risking everything." She shook her head, her eyes becoming glossy, betraying the fear she was trying to hide.

The fog seemed to press in on them, droplets of rain

sprinkling the space between them. It felt like their world was closing in.

"I don't have all the answers," he said. "But I'm willing to find them, together."

She paused, her chest rising and falling, like the tide around them. She gripped the edge of her jacket, looking for anything to anchor her in this moment. Neither of them could walk away now.

"Then we'll figure it out," she whispered.

***

Newport, Rhode Island, Present Day: Wes

When he returned to Susan's, he found clean scrubs in his dresser drawer and quickly changed into them, his mind racing a mile a minute. He grabbed his pager, which was sitting on his nightstand. Once he secured it on his hip and turned it on, it sprang to life. He checked the small screen and saw one name he recognized all too well.

Angie Stillman.

"Shit, no!" he yelled, racing down the stairs out to his car as quickly as he could.

As Wes ran up the steps to the entrance of the hospital, he could not fathom what he was about to encounter. He didn't know if Angie was having complications with the chemo or if it was her Leukemia progressing negatively.

He jumped into the elevator as his breathing increased. He couldn't help but think something was wrong. He thought of her last scan and reviewed it again in his head. Did he overlook something? He had looked over it several times.

His adrenaline was pumping as the elevator doors

opened. As soon as he could, he sprang forward towards the nursing station in the pediatric oncology unit.

"Where is she?" he shouted.

"Room four," the nurses replied, knowing too well who he was referring to.

"Talk to me," he demanded, entering her room. Dr. Gregory was calm as he placed the breathing tube down her throat.

"We need to open her airway," he stated, "and you can't be in here without the proper PPE," he reminded him.

"What a hazmat suit?" he asked sarcastically, "I'm fine!"

"Her airway closed," he said, placing the tube securely down her throat. The ventilator would breathe for her, giving her lungs a chance to stabilize. Her lifeless, tired body lay limp in the bed, her skin a pale sort of color, and her blues more blue than they ought to be.

"Seriously, Wes, you don't even have a mask on. Get out of here," he instructed. Wes backed up towards the door, his fingers fumbling for the handle while his eyes stayed glued to the bed. "Her oxygen was dropping, and she wasn't responding to steroids or breathing treatments."

"Shit. Where's her family?" he asked, looking around.

"In the waiting room." He hardly looked up as he went over her stats and checked every line again.

"Are you good here?" Wes grabbed a mask and shielded his mouth with it.

"Are you kidding?" he asked, "I'm pretty good at what I do, Wes."

"No need to be cocky right now. Don't let her plummet,"

he said, walking out of the room.

Dr. Gregory scoffed as if he had any say in the matter. They both understood that once a patient was put on a vent, the chances of them coming off it were slim.

***

Newport, Rhode Island, Present Day: Charlotte

The soft patter of the raindrops on the cobblestone streets was the only sound Charlotte could hear as she strolled down the street of the waterfront. She walked slowly, her hands tucked into the pockets of her raincoat. Her collar was turned up to shield her neck from the raindrops that fell off her pink umbrella. The clouds were a dark gray as the rain fell, almost hesitantly, like they, too, were unsure of where to fall. As she walked, she dodged the large puddles, taking her time glancing into the windows of the boutique shops that lined the water's edge. The town felt quiet, as if it were holding its breath alongside her.

She still wasn't sure what to make of Wes's decision.

Charlotte decided to duck into one of her favorite bookstores. As she entered, she lowered her umbrella, exposing herself to the rain for a brief moment. Tiny droplets of rain slid down her cheeks, like uninvited tears, as she entered the store. The doorbell chimed softly, as if she were being introduced to all the leather spined books that awaited her. The air smelled of leather and old paper, a scent that comforted her. The shop was dimly lit, the shelves towering over her in every direction, packed with books that felt like they had lived a million lives. The rain that now blustered outside tapped the windows, a soft rhythm filling the air.

As she walked up and down the aisles, she allowed her fingers to run across the spines of the books. Some were smooth, some were cracked, and some so well-worn that the titles were nearly invisible. The dark mahogany leather books caught her eye as she rounded the corner. She stopped to inspect them, her eyes trailing up and down the covers of each one. She thumbed through its pages, flipping through, but the words blurred as her thoughts drifted.

Wes.

She thought of his smile, the way his eyes lit up when he spoke of something he was passionate about. She thought of the way she felt when he was near her, the protection he offered so freely and effortlessly to those he cared about. The way he listened intently when she spoke made her feel seen, like she'd been found, after feeling lost for so long.

As the rain drizzled outside, she couldn't shake the feeling that had taken root inside her chest. A gnawing discomfort sat there, heavy with a weight she couldn't remove.

He's leaving her for me.

The thought echoed through the aisles of books, a painful truth she couldn't ignore. He's leaving the woman he's promised himself to, the life they'd built together, to possibly start something new. While her heart began to race at the possibilities of what that might look like, there was a quiet ache that followed. As if she was taking something from someone who never asked for this.

She ran her thumb over the spine of another book, the leather supple and new. The idea of something or someone being so well cared for, then passed over for something new, something unknown. The metaphor stung as she moved along, passing a few customers. Their footsteps were faint on the old wooden floor as she retreated further into the shadows of the shelves, as though she could hide from her thoughts running through her mind. She noticed a book teetering on the ledge of the shelf, its title smeared with age. She flipped through its pages, absentmindedly. Some of the pages had yellowed, some cracked at their edges, yet there was something beautiful about the way it sat in her hands. The promise of untold stories inside, just waiting to be discovered.

She felt a knot tighten in her stomach as she wondered about Emily, the woman he was leaving behind. Years of memories and laughter, he was handing back to her. Did she deserve this? Did she deserve her life torn apart? She knew the answer but was afraid to face the reality of their situation. Guilt began to seep into her bones like the rain onto fabric. She thought of Emily in Wes's apartment, gathering her things to leave.

Charlotte turned another corner, finding herself in the poetry section. The words on the pages here felt simpler, more direct than the thoughts swirling in her head. She picked up a collection of love poems and flipped through the delicate pages, stopping at the one title that caught her eye: *Love's Betrayal*. The irony wasn't lost on her. She placed it back on the shelf, her hand lingering on the spine longer than she intended. She wasn't sure why she was clinging to something as fragile as a book when her emotions were as raw as the storm outside. There was something comforting about being surrounded by thousands of books, though, whose worlds had been lived in before. Millions of characters whose lives were based off their authors, filled with conflict and confusion, much like her own. She didn't feel alone here.

She plucked another book from the poetry section, cradling it in her hands. She allowed herself to imagine a future with Wes. A life where the guilt they felt didn't exist. Where they found their own happiness, beyond the messy and imperfect start to their relationship. Her finger lingered on a page as she felt torn between the excitement of a new love and the impossible reality of the lives she never meant to disrupt.

With a sigh, she made her way towards the front of the store, unraveling the tie on her umbrella. She opened it up as she walked outside, the bitter chill of the breeze nipping her nose.

***

Newport, Rhode Island, Present Day: Wes

"Is she okay?" Mrs. Stillman begged as Wes strode toward them.

"I came as soon as I got paged," Wes explained. "We don't know much yet; all I know is that they had to put her on a vent to stabilize her airway."

Mrs. Stillman melted into her husband's arms, and her eyes filled with tears. Mr. Stillman's lip wavered, but he pulled his shoulders back and drew a long breath. "We had no idea. She complained of a headache, but we just figured that it was from chemo."

"She mentioned she was nauseous and didn't want to eat," Mrs. Stillman added.

"No fever though?" Wes asked, rubbing his chin.

They paused, rethinking every last detail of the last

few days. "She did feel warm the other night," her dad said. "But we just figured it was from chemo. We didn't even take her temperature."

"It's hard to differentiate," Wes sympathized. "The problem is, we don't know how this will progress."

"So what do we do?" they asked.

"We will monitor and treat symptoms as best we can. I will keep you updated, but she will definitely be admitted and kept here as of now."

He turned and made his way back into the unit. Dr. Gregory was at the nurses' station on a computer.

"How's she doing?" he asked.

Dr. Gregory leaned over his charts, thumbing through them with a frown that grew heavier with every flip. His dark hair fell disheveled over his forehead, and by the slope under his eye, he had been in for a long shift. As Wes approached, he pushed his files away.

"Stable for now, but we both have seen the trend with these patients on ventilators," he reminded Wes.

"She's going to be different," Wes said, walking past him. He took Angie's case very seriously. Maybe it was because she reminded him of someone from his past.

His little sister.

Charlotte was sitting outside on the front steps with her journal as Wes got home. He grasped the railing with white knuckles and dragged himself up until he was at Charlotte's feet, only then realizing her. He blinked a few times.

"Hey," She shut her leather-bound journal and set it to one side, looking up at him.

"Hey," He sighed, taking a seat next to her. He was

still in his scrubs as he tossed his white coat behind him. "Whatcha doing?"

"Writing. I've heard it helps process emotions, so I'm giving it a try." She rested her head on her hands to look at him fully. His clothes were wrinkled, but it was his eyes that concerned her most. Lifeless, like he was merely going through the motions. "How are you?"

He grunted in reply, "There are bad days and really bad days. This was one of the really bad ones." He rubbed his eyes before taking another sigh. "Where's my grandma?"

"Taking a nap," Charlotte said. "Is there anything I can do to help?"

"Have you cured cancer?"

She tapped the notebook. "Any day now."

He gave the barest smile before turning his gaze up the street, his glazed eyes trailing the people who passed by.

"You want to talk about it?" she asked, gently nudging him.

It took a few lingering seconds for him to notice. "No, I'm fine."

"Yeah, you seem fine," she responded, her words laced with sarcasm.

"I love my job, I do," he started to explain. "But sometimes I think my heart is too big for it."

Charlotte paused, letting him finish.

"I got into medicine because of my little sister," he explained.

"You have a sister?" she asked.

"*Had* a sister," he exhaled.

Charlotte's eyes fell on her shoes.

"It's okay, I was a kid when it happened," he clarified.

"What did she pass from?" Charlotte asked, taking great care in her word choice.

"Leukemia. All I remember is her coming home from chemo treatments, asleep on the couch. My parents were always fussing over her, trying to keep her comfortable. She was six years old when she passed away."

"I'm so sorry," Charlotte murmured.

"So, I made her my reason. I was determined to help any kid I could."

"It's your way of healing," she said.

"If I could cure just one kid from cancer, it would be enough," he answered.

"You are enough," Charlotte reminded him. "It's so hard to see in the day-to-day race of it all, but you are."

Wes smiled and looked into her eyes, her sincerity pouring out of them. He knew being in this specialty was going to be tough; he just had to learn not to take each obstacle personally. After all, these were his *patients*, not his *family*.

"I have an idea," Charlotte insisted, standing up to walk inside.

Wes had no idea what she was about to do until she walked back out with his guitar.

"A private concert just for me?" he asked.

"Hah! No, *you're* going to play. I noticed you when you were singing at the Wharf a few times. Playing seemed to calm you. It might cheer you up," she said, taking a seat back on the stoop, handing the guitar to Wes.

He started strumming a soft melody, his head swaying side to side with every note; his eyes shut as if her presence unfocused him.

Charlotte beamed, but it was when he opened his mouth to sing that it took her breath away. His soft but deep raspy voice drew her in. He wasn't singing loudly, but just loud enough for both of them to hear.

"You're really good," Charlotte said.

"Nah," he said in between notes.

She watched him play for a little while as her eyes drifted up the street. She forgot, for a moment, that their lives were laced in confusion. His melody seemed to mask her anxieties about the current state of their reality.

"If I were a melody, what would I sound like?" she asked.

"Oh, you?" Wes laughed, "Give me a minute."

As he thought, he chuckled to himself, smiling at her.

"If you were a melody, you would sound something like this."

She watched as his hands slowly moved up and down the neck of the guitar, as if he were massaging it. Her heart swelled at the thought of his hands sweeping across her body.

"That's beautiful," she said.

"Then I was correct."

He played for several more minutes, filling the silence between them and the darkening night sky. Fireflies began to float amidst the flickering streetlights.

Charlotte leaned her head back and closed her eyes. She felt invincible as the notes passed through her ears. She suddenly felt a cool raindrop fall on the bridge of her nose. She opened her eyes to Wes as he looked up at the sky. As the raindrops fell harder, they both stepped up to face the front door, anticipation growing in their hearts. Charlotte stopped as her hand rested on the doorknob, glancing behind to Wes. He paused behind her, the tension between them palpable. Charlotte's heart was pounding out of her chest.

"Wait," Wes said.

He didn't wait for her to respond. He wrapped one arm around her waist, forcing her to take a step downward. He placed his other hand on the curve of her jaw, drawing her lips closer to his. Charlotte was surprised at how natural it felt to kiss him. She drew her hand up and placed it on his chest. His tongue swiped across hers with such finesse that she craved more, not wanting it to end. He noticed the soft moan that leapt from her mouth. He pulled away first, staring into her eyes, longing for more.

"This complicates things," Charlotte said, looking up into his eyes.

"It's already complicated," he said.

***

Newport, Rhode Island, Present Day: Wes

The kitchen smelled of cinnamon and fresh bread as Wes sat across from Susan. Her weathered hands worked the Snickerdoodle dough, kneading it with much confidence, only decades of experience could provide. The kitchen was warm and cozy as sunlight streamed in through the windows, too warm for the icy chill that crept through his chest. He wasn't sure how this conversation was going to go. Susan could be a bit of a wild card.

"Grandma, we need to talk," Wes said, his voice strained.

Susan paused mid-knead, her sharp eyes flicking to his. "Oh, that tone," she muttered with a raised eyebrow. "You're not breaking up with me, too, are you? I've got too much invested in this relationship. You know too much," she laughed.

Wes laughed softly, grateful for her attempt at humor, "No," he said.

Susan set the dough aside, wrapping it in plastic wrap and placing it in the refrigerator to chill. "Well, spit it out then. You're looking like you've swallowed a live eel, and I'm too old to deal with that kind of drama without a cup of tea."

Wes raked his hands through his wavy hair. "I'm in love with Charlotte."

A smile curled at the corners of Susan's mouth. "I know," she said.

He took a deep breath, his gaze falling to his hands. "I know it sounds crazy after knowing Emily my whole life, but Charlotte just walked into our world and cleared my head. It feels like, with her around, everything clicked into place. I don't know how else to describe it."

There was a long silence as Susan listened, her eyes twinkling at her grandson. "Well, finally." Susan's voice broke the tension. "About time you came to your senses."

Wes' eyes widened. "Wait, you knew?"

Susan gave him a pointed look. "I'm your grandmother. I've known since the first time I saw you two together. I've been watching you two dance around each other for months."

He opened his mouth to speak, but paused. "I wanted to be respectful of Emily," he said.

Susan leaned forward. "Look, I'm not saying Emily is

a bad person, but if I'm being honest, she was never right for you." She rolled her eyes. "Hell, she's like a store bought pie."

"What?" Wes chuckled.

"She looks perfect and beautiful from the outside, but once you take a bite, you realize it's all fluff and no substance."

Wes snorted, choking on his own breath. "Grandma, you can't say that."

Susan held her nose high in the air. "I just did," she said. "I'm old, I've earned it."

Wes stared at her, his heart pounding.

"I am a little surprised you didn't come to me first. You usually always do."

Wes sighed, knowing this was coming. "I know, I just needed to make this decision on my own. I know we always agree, but I wanted to be sure for my own sake."

Susan's eyes twinkled. "Then you're making the right choice, Wes. Life's messy. Love is messy. But that's where all the good stuff lies," she said.

Wes laughed, a genuine, relieved smile blossomed across his face. "Thanks, Grandma, for everything."

"You're welcome," she said. "Next time I let a stray in, it won't be a beautiful woman," she chuckled. "Just promise me something," she said.

"Anything," he said.

"Don't you dare show up with any more store-bought pie."

"I wouldn't dream of it," Wes said, standing up to leave.

Susan waved him off with a grin. "Go get your girl."

***

Newport, Rhode Island, Present Day: Wes & Emily

The chair grated against the ground as Wes pulled it out to sit. The sound put his nerves on edge. He messed with the napkin, adjusted the silverware, and checked the clock fifteen times before spotting Emily's dark hair and slender frame cautiously entering the restaurant. She'd chosen the location. An expensive place where tables were seated far away from each other, and privacy was guaranteed. If she hadn't suggested it, Wes would have.

Her hair was longer, and it was the first time in years they'd been apart long enough to notice a physical change in her. There was something different about how she walked, too. More reserved. Like she was holding herself in instead of wrapping herself around him after being apart for so long.

Wes stood as she neared, acutely aware of his emotions as they embraced. Waiting to see if his heart lurched for her again. It didn't. She withdrew stiffly and sat down, crossing one leg over the other and straightening her blazer like it'd been disrupted at his touch.

Wes sat with a sigh. "It's been a while."

She let out a small laugh, and it seemed to break some of the tension. "It has."

His back went rigid.

"You weren't lonely, though, were you?" she said, taking a long sip of the ice water in front of her.

His gaze flicked up. "What?" A waiter brought menus over, then read the air and quickly left. "What did you ask?"

Emily's lips trembled slightly as she spun her engagement ring around her left finger.

"Come on, Wes, we both know what's going on here," she said.

Wes swallowed hard. "There is something missing, if I'm being honest."

A small broken laugh escaped Emily's lips. "So this is it? All of the years we've spent together, you're just walking away?"

Wes nodded, his heart heavy. "I think we both know this is the right thing. We've been holding onto something that's gone."

Emily paused, her eyes widening. She began to blink rapidly, trying to steady herself.

"If we continued on, we might be fine, but I know deep down, we'd be holding each other back from the lives we know we deserve," he said.

Emily looked up, her eyes brimming with tears. She folded her hands on the white tablecloth as she took off her engagement ring and set it between them.

Wes stared at the diamond, empty promises gilded into the speckles of light shimmering from within the setting.

Emily sighed, "I think this belongs to you now."

Wes sat for a moment, his jaw tightening.

"Even after all of this, I'm going to miss you," she said.

Wes stood, embracing her in a long hug. Images of summers spent running outside playing hide and seek among the fireflies flashed across his mind; her laugh would forever be engrained into his heart. He thought of late nights under the stars as teenagers, holding onto her as tightly as he could, trying to preserve their moment in time.

"I wish you the world, Emily. I hope you know that."

With those words, it was like things were final. They settled over the two of them like a heavy flood, washing away what was once their relationship. Leaving a hollow feeling in its place. Emily looked to the ceiling as she pulled in a breath of air, then blew it out. "We grew up," she muttered.

She stood, relaxing into him one last time. Perhaps if they'd broken up months ago, there would have been a fight, but now, it'd been so long that there was hardly anything to fight for. His head rested on the top of hers.

"I'm sorry," he whispered, kissing the crown of her head.

"Me too," she exhaled, her body falling into his, his arms wrapped firmly around her. She nuzzled into his chest.

The harbor was quiet as the evening rolled in. The Goat Island lighthouse shone across the bay, signaling to boaters that darkness was falling around them.

***

Newport, Rhode Island, Present Day: Charlotte

As Charlotte walked towards the Wharf to meet her boss for a drink, she couldn't help but wonder what Wes was up to. Although they had both hinted at their feelings for one another, they hadn't talked about what the future held. Susan mentioned he had picked up more shifts at the hospital, throwing himself into work. She knew they needed to talk soon, though.

The main street was alive with the soft hum of a lazy afternoon. The little cafe on the corner was filled with chatter from locals, the clinking of glasses, and the smell of something sweet dancing in the air.

The cobblestone pathway met her feet as she grew closer to their meeting spot, but as she glanced around the Wharf, something else caught her eye. Two people were embracing one another, the glass window exposing them to all of Newport.

For a moment, her world seemed to slow. Her breath hitched in her throat as her heart dropped into her stomach. She knew those tattoos; she had admired them for months.

Wes.

She watched as he kissed a woman on the top of her head, folding his strong arms around her. Charlotte had been the one he had held before; she remembered the warmth he exuded. His strength was once her haven as they lived in the unknown together. The woman turned her face to the side, a silhouette Charlotte could not ignore.

Emily.

A pang of jealousy surged through her, catching her off guard. She hadn't known Emily was back in town. Last she heard, she was in Martha's Vineyard at their family's second home. She tried to move, but her legs wouldn't allow it. Her chest felt heavy, and the oxygen was trapped in her lungs. Her eyes tried to look away from them, but they wouldn't budge. All confidence she had of his feelings towards her was now adrift to the sea. She watched as they slowly departed from one another. She gazed at them as she watched him pull his hand up around her cheeks, holding her face ever so gently in his hands.

It suddenly felt like everything that had transpired between them over the last few months was slowly seeping back into the sand. She turned, about to leave, but her eyes were fixed on his hands curling around her waist, holding her. Her hands were straight at her sides, and the sadness and confusion tightened around her chest. She hadn't expected to see Wes and Emily wrapped up in a lingering embrace. Were they reconciling? It sure didn't look as if they were breaking up. Frustration straightened her spine, propelling her forward. She needed to be somewhere, anywhere else. With her mind swirling, she walked away.

***

Newport, Rhode Island, Present Day: Wes

Wes felt Charlotte's presence before he saw her, a shift in the air. He glanced out the window and saw *her*. She was outside, just a few steps away, standing on the sidewalk. She was looking down at her phone, unaware of his meeting with Emily. *The meeting* was where he was single-handedly changing the trajectory of his life.

The thing was, he didn't want Charlotte to see him like this, with Emily still in his arms. He didn't want Charlotte to think he was still tethered to his old life.

His stomach twisted as he pulled away from Emily and sat down in his chair. His eyes were locked on Charlotte's form, even though she had no idea he was looking.

"I'm not really in the mood to eat," Emily said.

Wes's eyes snapped back to Emily, but only for a moment. Emily looked down at the menu, her nose half up in the air. He took advantage of the opportunity and darted his eyes back to the window, scanning the street outside. But there was nothing. Had she seen him?

A part of him wanted to leave the table to run after

Charlotte, but he didn't. He wanted to tell her everything and explain how it was over; he had left Emily. Yet, he knew Emily deserved this moment. She deserved his time, even if it meant shattering both of their worlds in a quiet, agonizing way.

"I think I just want a cocktail," Emily muttered, picking up the slender drink menu.

"Sounds good," Wes said.

The amber glow of the low-hanging pendant lights cast soft shadows on Emily's face. The spark she once had in her eyes had gone dull, as if the tide had retreated from the shores of her spirit. His eyes studied her for the last time, as if she were a place he would never return to. He noticed the delicate arch of her eyebrow and the softness of her mauve lips. Her fingers, once intertwined with his, now rested on the rim of her glass, tracing absent circles.

"I always loved this place," she said. "It's so quiet."

"We came here for our first date," Wes said.

Emily looked up at him as her lips curled into a small, reluctant smile. The memory was warm but felt distant. He watched her sip her drink, the curve of her neck as she tilted her glass back, the way her hair fell in soft waves on her shoulders.

"Emily…" his voice cracked as he cleared his throat.

"You don't have to explain anything," she said. "I can't just…let go. Not like it's nothing, but I will if you need me to."

Wes's chest pinched as he exhaled, feeling the weight of the moment. It wasn't nothing, it never had been.

He would always have love for her. The kind that roared in the storms and whispered in the stillness of the calm. He had known her in a way that no one else ever would.

He had had a front row seat to her childhood, and he watched her grow into the woman who sat before him. Her quiet laugh, the way her eyes fluttered shut when she was trying to remember details of a forgotten memory.

"I just want you to know," he said. "This breakup, for me, was a lot like the tide. It started off slow, barely noticeable, but then it took everything with it. And as much as I wanted to pull it all back, sometimes life just kept pulling us apart. I wish I could have stopped it, but I can't change the way the current moves."

He could almost feel the rhythm of the waves in his heart. His words hung between them like a mist rising above the harbor at dawn. Emily's eyes softened as a tear slid down her cheek, catching the light of the sun lowering in the sky. She was glowing, as though she were already slipping away from him, leaving behind only a shadow of who she had been in his life.

The ocean had pulled them in, had worn them down with its tides. Now, it was pulling them apart.

"I'm not who you need anymore, and that has to be okay," she muttered.

Wes reached across the table and enveloped her hand in his.

With that, the door between their old life and whatever new thing might exist silently swung shut.

Chapter 17

Newport, Rhode Island, Present Day: Charlotte

Charlotte's eyes fluttered open as she awoke, her arms outstretched above her. Her eyes watched as relentless sheets of rain drowned out all other sound, tapping on her window, as if the world had slipped into a sorrowful dream.

"You're up early," Susan welcomed her in the kitchen, looking up from her crossword puzzle.

"It looks nasty out," Charlotte said, glancing out the bay windows.

"So," Susan said with a raised eyebrow, her voice light yet laced with a sharp edge that only comes from years of seeing people hide their true feelings. "Tell me, love, what is going on between you and my grandson?" Susan set her puzzle down, the newspaper crinkling in her hands.

Charlotte swallowed hard, feeling the weight of her question. Ashamed yet unable to deny the truth, she said, "I...I think we have feelings for each other."

Susan took another sip of her piping hot tea, its steam curling above her mug. She peered at Charlotte with a knowing smile, "Complicated, eh? Is that the term you young people are using these days for 'it's a total mess'?"

Susan chuckled at her own joke, but Charlotte couldn't seem to muster a smile. Instead, words spewed out of her mouth, "He's engaged. I know it's wrong, and he does too. I never wanted to fall for him, I promise. That was never a part of the plan. Now he's talking about leaving her, and I don't know what to do with that."

Susan's expression shifted from playful to serious, her eyes sharpening for a moment. Her fingers tapped the edge of her mug, letting the awkward silence fill the space between them. She had already known this from Wes's confession, but thought she'd play along.

"You're telling me, my grandson, the one who *can't* make a decision without asking me ten times for advice, has somehow managed to fall for you, and is also planning on leaving Emily?" Susan raised her eyebrow, her tone a perfect mixture of skepticism and intrigue. "Well, well, well…that is a bit of a pickle, isn't it?"

Charlotte nodded, her body still. "I know all of this is wrong. We both do."

Susan leaned back in her chair and folded her arms across her chest. Her voice softened just a bit, "Love does tend to have that effect on people, makes us all act like fools. Makes us do things we shouldn't do."

Charlotte's eyes lifted to Susan's, feeling a mixture of disbelief and frustration. "You think this is okay?"

Susan let out a small laugh, "Oh, sweetheart, I didn't say that, but I will *not* miss Emily. What I'm also trying to say is that the road to love is not always paved and pretty, and it sure as hell doesn't follow any rulebook. But don't you dare tell me this isn't something that's been in the air from the beginning. You two. *I've seen it.*"

Charlotte blinked. "What do you mean?"

"At the Wharf during open mic nights, at the Fourth of July party," Susan took a deep breath and placed a hand on Charlotte's, her eyes twinkling with mischief, "The way he looks at you, like nobody else exists—don't try to tell me otherwise. I know my grandson."

"But what about Emily? How is she going to take all of this? She already hates me," Charlotte sighed.

Susan folded her hands on the table with a surprising gentleness, "You're not the villain here, love. Sometimes life puts us in these...difficult situations. It's not about being good or bad. It's about what you do next. What you both decide to do with what's in front of you. Don't mistake guilt for the real issue here. The real issue is whether or not love is something worth fighting for. That's what I want you two to think about."

Charlotte's mind swirled and swayed.

Susan leaned in as if to tell her a secret, "I'm not saying it's going to be easy. Hell, nothing worth having comes easy. But what I do know is this. If he is willing to leave her for you, then there's something real there. Don't you dare dismiss that."

Charlotte let Susan's words sink in, feeling both relieved and terrified. Susan didn't judge her; rather, she gave her permission to explore her feelings. Even though it was messy.

"Sometimes a little mess is exactly what we need to make something real," she explained, filling her teacup.

Charlotte chuckled, feeling the weight of their decisions slowly slide off her shoulders, "I'll keep that in mind."

"Good, now go talk to him. Life's too damn short to

wait for the perfect moment."

"Do you know where he is?" she asked.

"Mainsail."

***

Newport, Rhode Island, Present Day: Wes & Charlotte

The morning sun was soft and golden, a slight breeze swaying the trees that skirted the cobblestone pathways. He watched as leaves pirouetted to the ground, their edges browning as autumn slowly approached. The faint sound of seagulls echoed in the distance as Wessat at a small outside table in front of Mainsail. He sipped his coffee as his eyes were fixated on the boats that drifted toward the horizon, lost in thought. His phone sat forgotten beside him, the buzz of incoming messages ignored. He had been there for over an hour, thinking and journaling, as if that could bring relief to his situation. It was quiet and peaceful, and yet, his heart felt anything but at ease.

Charlotte walked along Thames Street, her steps quick and purposeful. She knew she needed to take Susan's advice and really allow herself a chance to explain her feelings to Wes. He deserved that, too, especially since he was the one changing the course of his life. She knew they should have had this conversation sooner, but the words had been stuck in her throat, tangled with doubts and fear. She turned the corner and caught sight of him, alone. Her heart jolted in her chest as she walked toward him. Wes's sweater sleeves were rolled up, his hair looking a little disheveled but still handsome. She drew in a deep breath and walked toward him, trying to steady her nerves.

Wes heard leaves rustling close to him and lifted his gaze from his journal to *her*, Charlotte. His heart gave a quick, almost painful thud in his chest. He hadn't expected to see her, not yet.

"Hey," he said softly, his voice a little rough from the weight of his thoughts.

Charlotte stopped in front of him, the words she had rehearsed on the walk down to him tumbling out of her mouth, "Susan had mentioned you were here, and I was hoping to have a word with you."

Wes chuckled lightly. There was a flicker of sadness in his eyes, "I come here a lot, sitting here helps me think."

Charlotte nodded, her heart pounding.

"Please, have a seat," he said.

"I'm sorry," she said, sitting across from him. " I can't hold this back anymore. I have to say what's on my mind, even if this is one of the hardest things I've ever done."

Wes sat up straight, frowning a little.

"I have real feelings for you, big feelings," she said. "I realize there are a million things to consider about this whole situation, but I need you to know I can't deny it, not anymore. If you have changed your mind, I get it. You don't have to see me anymore."

Wes' eyes widened. His mouth opened to speak, but no sound came out. His mind was reeling, wondering if this moment was actually happening.

Charlotte reached out, placing her hand on his. "You don't have to say anything yet. I just needed you to know, you needed to hear the truth from me."

For a moment, they both sat there, the world around

them fading into the morning sun. The quiet tension between them thickened, slowly shrinking the space between them.

Wes reached out his hand, gently cupping her cheek. He looked at her, his eyes full of wonder and something deeper, "I only ever want to see you," he said, his thumb brushing her skin lightly. "I left her."

***

Newport, Rhode Island, Present Day: Charlotte

Charlotte was sitting in the living room flipping through the television channels. She stopped at the news station, hoping for the best. Susan had gone to bed a few hours prior, and Wes was at the hospital. She slinked down the couch cushion, covering her body with the throw blanket. As she watched the news, she folded her arms, holding the blanket close. Her eyes became heavy until she succumbed to her tiredness and fell asleep.

An hour or two later, Wes stumbled through the door. He glanced around the room but didn't see anybody. He figured his grandmother and Charlotte had already gone to bed. He moved past the family room and into the dining room adjacent to the laundry room. There, he peeled off his scrubs and instantly threw them in the wash, in hopes of containing the germs he knew were all over them. He undressed and turned the washing machine on, only wearing his boxers. He turned to walk up the stairs when suddenly he froze on the first step. Charlotte was cozied up, asleep on the couch. He smiled as he watched her face, so peaceful as her chest slowly moved up and down. She moved her head to the side, exposing her bare neck, her tank top hugging her chest. He remembered her complaining of neck pain the last time she had fallen asleep on the couch, and he didn't want that to happen again. So he walked over to the couch, extending his arms and picking her up. She didn't move; she was deeply asleep. He carefully walked up the stairs, the wood creaking beneath his feet. He quietly nudged her bedroom door open with his foot as he walked in, still holding firmly to her petite body. Once at her bed, he carefully placed her head on her pillow, the rest of her body instantly engulfed by the pillowy mattress beneath her. As his arms pulled away from under her, he noticed her eyes flutter open.

"I just thought this might be more comfortable," he whispered with a smile. "Go back to sleep."

Charlotte wasn't sure if it was a dream or if this was her reality, but she didn't care. As he turned to walk away, she grabbed his hand, pulling him back toward her.

"Do you need anything?" he asked, moving dangerously close to her, his face inches from hers.

"You," she smiled, hazily.

She wrapped her arms around his neck as he collapsed onto her. She felt his robust chest on hers, his body warmth radiating.

"Charley," he whispered, cautioning.

She stopped him from talking, kissing his lips as slowly as she could. She wanted to savor this moment, not sure where it would lead.

He pulled his hands up, one on her cheek as they kissed, and another to hold himself up. She caressed his bare chest, her fingers drifting along his tattoos. He felt his body tingle with every touch. He kissed her harder, with much passion. She kissed back, matching his exuberance.

"You sure?" he asked, pulling away.

"Stop talking," she smiled, pulling him back.

Their bodies moved together like the tide drifting to and from shore. With each breath, they kissed endlessly, inching closer to one another but never being close enough. He was her guiding light as she followed his lead.

His touch was strong, yet gentle.

His body was toned, yet soft.

He pulled her on top of him as she removed her tank top, exposing herself. He stopped and stared at her with wonder, a sleepy smile slapped onto his face. She bent down to kiss him as he grabbed the small of her back, his hands trickled up her spine as they moved together as one. Wes moved her back onto the bed as he took control, never leaving her lips. He entered her slowly. Her whole body shivered.

"Are you okay?" he asked.

"Yes," she nodded, their breathing both becoming shallower.

Her lips were secured onto his cheek, her body becoming a slave to his.

He knew exactly what he was doing, she thought.

After several minutes had passed, she felt an eruption brewing inside of her. It was growing with every breath, with every movement of his hips. She could tell he was close, too, the sweat on his brow gleaming in the moonlight through her bedroom window. Together, they held each other as they both surrendered. Wes slowly collapsed next to her, continuing to kiss her as she came down from her high as well. Several moments went by, and both their breaths returned to a normal rhythm as a giggle expelled from her throat. He stroked her stomach, a single finger making circles around her belly button. Wes smiled and held her close. He noticed her toes and fingers were warm to the touch.

"How are you feeling?" he asked.

She didn't respond; she just smiled with her eyes closed.

There were no words to describe how she was feeling, she

thought.

Charlotte turned to her side as Wes moved behind her. His arms were secure under their shared pillow and around her waist. His chin was nuzzled into the nape of her neck, tickling her skin with every breath. They closed their eyes, drifting off to sleep, together at last.

"Charley!" Debbie called, snapping Charlotte back to reality, like a rope pulling taut after it's been slack for too long.

The world around her suddenly felt louder, clearer, as if she'd just resurfaced from being underwater. She blinked hard, shaking off the lingering warmth of her daydream, feeling a rush of embarrassment flood her cheeks.

She turned and saw Debbie walk into the store, her back straightening in her chair at the counter at Finnegan's.

"Hey!" Charlotte said, brushing a strand of hair that had fallen across her face.

***

Newport, Rhode Island, Present Day: Charlotte & Emily

After her shift at the store, Charlotte decided to run some errands. She wandered into the small local bookstore, the kind of place where peace existed among the old leather spines of books left untouched. As she stood frozen, flipping through the pages of a book she'd never buy, her calm was suddenly shattered by a voice that sent a chill up her spine.

"Well, well, if it isn't Newport's newest homewrecker."

Charlotte's head snapped up, her heart stumbling in her chest. She couldn't have been more wrong about how pleasant her evening was going to be. Wes was going to be at

Susan's house, and a promise of a hearty homemade dinner awaited her. However, standing a few feet away, with her arms crossed over her chest, was Emily.

She had a presence that demanded attention, not necessarily in a good way. Tall and polished, with her sleek hair that looked like it had been professionally done. Her lips were a bold red, one that always meant business. She looked Charlotte up and down, sizing her up.

Charlotte felt her cheeks become rosy-pink, but she smiled, trying to keep things light. She wanted to pretend like she was meeting an old acquaintance unexpectedly, not the woman whose life had been upended by the man Charlotte had fallen for. However, Charlotte wasn't about to be called a homewrecker.

"Charlotte," she corrected her, extending her hand a little too eager.

Emily's eyes flicked briefly to Charlotte's hand before she ignored it, her smile cool. "I know," she muttered. "I've been hearing a lot about you around town lately."

"I think this town's been kind to me so far," Charlotte replied, with a softness that felt like a challenge.

"You think so?" Emily asked. She let the question hang between them, her eyes narrowing, her expression thinly veiled with a condescension.

There was something so conniving about the way Emily had approached her. Charlotte tried to play devil's advocate. Her life had just been flipped upside down, of course she was going to loathe Charlotte. However, it felt like she was trying to test her, probing her for weaknesses so she could exploit it somehow. She moved like she had control.

"I see," Charlotte said, "I hope good things."

"Oh, mostly," she said, with an edge that bit the tension in the air.

Charlotte's feet shifted beneath her. "There are so many nice people, I've been really lucky," she said.

Emily's lips tightened, and Charlotte could almost hear the snap of her patience fraying at the edges. "I'm sure you've gotten to know Wes pretty well now," she said, her tone sharp.

"Yes, he and Susan are wonderful," she said.

"He's really good at making people feel comfortable; he's always been that way. I just wonder how long that charm will last," Emily said, her tone almost sweet.

The words landed like bricks on Charlotte's shoulders. She was trying to provoke her, to somehow get a reaction out of her. Like, somehow it would validate whatever thoughts she was trying to hold onto about Wes.

"Look, I know what you're trying to do, Emily, but I promise that whatever happened between you and Wes was not on purpose or done by me. I don't want to fight," Charlotte said, her voice steady.

For a split second, Emily's face softened, like she was almost surprised by the straightforwardness of Charlotte's words. But then, just as quickly, she masked it with a sharp smile. "Oh, I'm not fighting with you," she said, her voice sugary sweet. "I'm just amazed at how one person can move in, take over a small town such as Newport, and charm everybody in it."

Charlotte's lips parted, but she caught herself just in time. This was the part where she could easily get defensive and let Emily win. But instead, she grinned and said, "I'm not here to take over anything, Emily. I just want to enjoy my life."

There it was. The deafening moment of silence. Emily's expression was unrecognizable, and Charlotte was unsure how she would respond. For the first time, Charlotte felt she had the upper hand.

Emily's eyes flickered, her nose raising upward. "Well, good luck with that," she muttered, before turning on her heel and walking away. Her heels clicked sharply against the wooden floor, the air choppy with tension.

Charlotte exhaled slowly, her shoulders sagging with relief. She had never liked confrontation, certainly not with Emily. But now, the awkwardness felt freeing.

"Well, that was *something*," she whispered to herself with a wry smile.

Once again, she was reminded that life in this small town, for all its charm, was never going to be simple.

***

Newport, Rhode Island, Present Day: Charlotte

"You'll never guess who I just ran into?" Charlotte asked, closing the door softly behind her, the smell of rosemary and thyme filling her nostrils.

The world outside felt like a distant echo.

"Oh no, who?" Susan asked, extending her arms for a hug.

"I just ran into Emily," she said. "At the bookstore on my way home."

Susan and Wes stared at each other, their gazes

unmatched.

"She definitely blames me for everything," Charlotte said, biting her lip and reaching for a wine glass.

Wes was standing by the counter, stirring whatever was in the pot on the stove. His expression was strained. "How'd it go?" he asked.

Charlotte forced a smile, even with the weight of her conversation with Emily still heavy on her chest. She wasn't sure how to start, but her gaze flicked to Susan, who was watching her with an unmistakable glint of curiosity.

"She tried to intimidate me, in her own special way," Charlotte said.

Wes was silent for a moment, his jaw tightening.

"Oh, for heaven's sake," Susan muttered, setting the salad bowl off to the side. "That woman's got some nerve."

Charlotte noticed Wes's hand clench, but his voice was calm and gentle as he approached her. "Did she say anything else?"

Charlotte nodded slowly. "She made it seem like I came here and ruined everything. Almost like things were fine before I showed up." She could feel the sting of Emily's words all over again, her chest squeezing with a mixture of frustration and disbelief.

"Don't let her get under your skin," Susan said. "She's just mad because the man she thought she could control didn't want to be."

Charlotte smiled at Susan's bluntness. "I don't know, Susan. She seemed to believe I was the one to cause all of this. Like I meant to."

Wes placed his hand on the small of Charlotte's back.

"This wasn't about you," he said.

Charlotte met his eyes, the weight of his words wrapping around her. Still, the doubt lingered. "She's still the one that's hurt," she said.

Susan snorted. "The only thing Emily's upset about is how you came into our lives and showed Wes what he's been missing."

There was no malice in Susan's words, just pure truth. Emily wasn't mad at Charlotte for *who* she was; she was mad that Charlotte had become the one thing that Emily had failed to be. The person Wes needed.

"I'm sorry you had to deal with that," Wes said, his voice softening as he spoke. "I need you to know none of this is your fault. We're here because of what we *feel* towards each other."

Charlotte's heart lurched at his words. She wanted to believe him, but still couldn't shake the blame she felt.

"Emily couldn't see what was right in front of her, and now she's mad because you came along and got the best of Wes," Susan explained, feeling the weight of the moment.

Charlotte stifled out a sigh. She looked up at Wes with steady eyes and felt a warmth seep back into her chest. There was no denying it now. Emily's bitterness wasn't about Charlotte. It was something deeper, something that Charlotte couldn't change.

Wes smiled, pulling her gently towards him. "You're not alone in this, Charlotte. We're here, together."

"Together," Charlotte repeated, the word settling in her chest like a promise.

And with that, the weight of the world seemed to fall

away, replaced by the warmth of Wes's steady hand and Susan's relentless humor. Whatever Emily had said didn't matter. She had found her place, here, with these two, and that was more than enough.

***

Newport, Rhode Island, Present Day: Wes & Charlotte

The bustling waterfront of the Wharf was lined with rows of tents and stands along the pier, each offering shucked oysters, clam chowder, and lobster rolls. The cool salty breeze brushed Charlotte's hair off her shoulders as the faint sound of a local band playing folk music danced between her ears. The air was thick with excitement as the annual Oyster Festival kicked off the start of the autumn season.

Charlotte pulled her soft, quilted coat up around her shoulders as they walked, hand in hand, into the crowd.

"Are you excited?" Wes asked, clasping his hand tightly around hers.

Charlotte nervously curled a strand of hair behind her ear. "Yes, just unsure of how everyone will react…to us."

Wes gave her hand a reassuring squeeze. "I wouldn't worry about that," he smiled.

Charlotte rolled her eyes as the corners of her cheeks flushed. There was a nervous flutter in her stomach as they weaved through the crowd, passing a few food stands on their way to a few of the picnic tables at the end of the dock. As they walked through, the scent of garlic butter and charred oysters filled their nostrils.

As they cleared the crowd, a group of Wes's friends was crowded around a picnic table. They were all laughing and holding half-shucked oysters, their chilled craft beers atop the table too. Ryan was the first to spot them as he turned around and waved enthusiastically. "Hey! You two made it!"

The rest of the group erupted with laughter as Wes and Charlotte approached them. Charlotte blushed at the rush of attention they were receiving, but Wes stayed next to her, his hand reassuringly resting on the small of her back.

"Charlotte, you know some of my high school friends," he said. "This is her first Oyster Fest."

"Well, welcome!" one of his friends said.

"Finally!" another exclaimed. "Glad you two are finally out here together."

"I agree with that statement!" a bold Piper exclaimed, emerging from the crowd with a drink in her hand, embracing Charlotte in a hug.

Wes leaned forward. "Thank you," he said.

Paul came over and handed Charlotte a freshly shucked oyster. "You have to have at least one. It's like a rite of passage."

Charlotte looked down at the gleaming shell with wide eyes. "I've never had one," she confessed.

"What?" they all seemed to say at once.

"You just have to do it fast," Piper explained. "And chase it with a sip of beer."

"It tastes better with some hot sauce," Wes said, squirting a small amount on the oyster.

Charlotte looked up at Wes and Piper, hesitantly.

"I promise, it's really good," Wes assured her.

Charlotte took a breath and knocked it back into her mouth, swallowing it all at once. Her face lit up with surprise.

"Okay. Wow. That's actually pretty good."

The group cheered as the playful atmosphere grew even more infectious.

Wes leaned in and whispered, "Want a beer?"

"Of course!" Charlotte said. "Surprise me."

Wes left her side as Charlotte mingled with Piper and their friend group. The sound of the sharp *shink* of knives against the shells filled the air. Charlotte couldn't deny the delight of this maritime tradition. The chatter of the crowds surrounding them mixed with the scent of fresh seafood and charcoal grills filled the air. The golden light from the setting sun danced across the water, turning the waves into ripples of gold. The festival tents were decorated with string lights, small lanterns, and bunting that fluttered in the salty wind. Wooden picnic tables were scattered about Bowen's Wharf, their tops dotted with open oyster shells and half-empty beer cans. Clusters of people huddled together, enjoying their food, catching up with friends and loved ones.

"Here you go," Wes smiled, handing her a can of cold beer.

"Thank you," she said, cradling it in her hands.

"So, how's it going so far? Loving it?" Wes asked, his gaze turning towards Charlotte, his eyes reflecting the soft colors of the sunset.

"Yes," she said. "As if this town could get any better."

Wes watched Charlotte as the wind gently tousled her hair. The breeze picked up, and she took a sip of her beer.

"It feels like we're on the edge of the world," she said, looking up at him, her nose pink from the breeze nipping its edge.

Wes stepped closer, the sound of the surrounding crowd quieting around them, replaced by the soft lapping of the waves hitting the pier. The golden light spilled across Charlotte's face as she blinked, her eyes wide with happiness.

"This town is small enough to know your name, but big enough to let you be. That's why I'll never leave, like it's supposed to be this way," he said, gesturing to the ocean and the boats docked at the pier.

"It's simple here, if you just stop and listen," she said.

Charlotte felt the weight of her words settle inside her bones. She glanced at the festival and then back to Wes, feeling a deep connection to not just him, but the earth beneath her feet.

As if on cue, a vendor called out from a nearby booth, offering a tray of freshly shucked oysters. The folk music strained in the distance as Wes pulled Charlotte closer to him. Charlotte hesitated for a moment, a playful smile sweeping across her face as she picked up an oyster. She raised it to Wes as if she were about to make a toast, "Here goes nothing!" She giggled, sliding the oyster into her mouth. The briny flavor burst on her tongue, her eyes a mixture of surprise and delight.

"Okay, I get what all the hype is about now," she said to Wes, leaning into him.

For a heartbeat, she could feel his breath on her neck, his body radiating warmth to hers. Then, without a word, his hand found her waist, pulling her gently against him, her back resting against his chest. His fingers skimmed across the top of her jeans as he secured her. A shock of electricity curled up her spine as she melted into him, her fingers briefly brushing across his hands that clung to her hips. Slowly, he tilted his head, his lips brushing the top of her head.

"You missed," she whispered.

She could almost instantly feel the steady thrum of his heartbeat.

"What do you mean?" he asked into her ear. His breath was steady, a quiet reassurance.

She turned to face him and lifted her lips to his.

"You missed," she repeated.

For a long moment, they stood there, the world slipping away until there was nothing left but the faint rustling of her breath mingling with his.

Her hand tightened slightly on his arm, inching him closer, instinctually craving his closeness. His warm hand, despite the chill in the air, clutched her jaw line ever so slightly as his lips met hers. There was nothing in the world that could change that feeling.

They had each other, and that was enough.

Bitsy Yates has spent over 10 years teaching English, where she's been lucky enough to share her love for storytelling with students while also growing as a writer herself. She earned her Bachelor's Degree from Radford University and a Master of Arts in Teaching Degree from Christopher Newport University, which set her on the path of combining her passions for education and writing. Bitsy lives in Virginia with her husband and two children, drawing constant inspiration from their love and support as she continues her writing journey.